"Are you sure that Rambo knows what he's doing?"

Andrew nodded. "If Rambo led us this way, it was for a reason. Lexi was down here."

"Then that settles it. Lexi was abducted."

"Why don't we sit down for a moment?" Andrew nodded to a large rock beside the creek.

Natalie nodded and lowered herself onto the cold stone.

Something gleamed below her. She reached between the rocks and picked up the object.

A hoop earring—just like the ones Lexi loved to wear.

Her stomach dropped. "Oh no."

"Is that your sister's?" Andrew asked.

"It looks like hers."

Losing an earring indicated to Natalie that a struggle had gone down.

She desperately wanted to reverse time back to when things were going well. Before walking in on the killings. Before Lexi had disappeared.

But she couldn't. Lexi being missing kept her in place—and maybe that was exactly what someone had planned...

Christy Barritt's books have won a Daphne du Maurier Award for Excellence in Suspense and Mystery and have been twice nominated for an RT Reviewers' Choice Best Book Award. She's married to her Prince Charming, a man who thinks she's hilarious—but only when she's not trying to be. Christy is a self-proclaimed klutz, an avid music lover and a road-trip aficionado. For more information, visit her website at christybarritt.com.

Books by Christy Barritt

Love Inspired Suspense

Visit the Author Profile page at LoveInspired.com.

LETHAL MOUNTAIN PURSUIT

CHRISTY BARRITT

LOVE INSPIRED SUSPENSE
INSPIRATIONAL ROMANCE

LOVE INSPIRED® SUSPENSE

INSPIRATIONAL ROMANCE

ISBN-13: 978-1-335-59792-2

Lethal Mountain Pursuit

Recycling programs
for this product may
not exist in your area.

This is a work of fiction. Names, characters, places and incidents are either the
product of the author's imagination or are used fictitiously. Any resemblance
to actual persons, living or dead, businesses, companies, events or locales is
entirely coincidental.

For questions and comments about the quality of this book, please contact us
at CustomerService@Harlequin.com.

Love Inspired
22 Adelaide St. West, 41st Floor
Toronto, Ontario M5H 4E3, Canada
www.LoveInspired.com

Printed in U.S.A.

But the Lord is faithful, who shall stablish you,
and keep you from evil.
—*2 Thessalonians* 3:3

Thank you to my home Bible study group
for always being there for me. Life is sweeter with you
all by my side. Scott; Monty and Robin; Rick and Carrie;
Steve and Nikki; Tyler and Stephanie; and Helza.

ONE

Natalie Pearson sat up straight in bed.

Sweat covered her forehead, and her heart pounded in her ears as fear gripped her.

What had that noise been?

Had the killer hunting her somehow followed her here?

Would this be his moment of reckoning? Where he'd finish what he started?

He'd almost taken her life two months ago.

The scar on her jaw throbbed at the reminder that she'd barely escaped.

She ignored the pain, instead listening for any telltale signs that the killer was close.

Quiet filled the air, and unmoving shadows clung to the darkness surrounding her.

Maybe she'd imagined the thump outside.

She'd been dealing with nightmares for months. Perhaps she'd only been dreaming.

Even as Natalie willed her racing heart to calm, she knew that wasn't the case.

She had come to her sister's little cabin nestled deep in the heart of the Tennessee woods, surrounded by the Smoky Mountains, so she could hide.

Lexi had said Natalie could come stay since she'd been having trouble paying the rent anyway.

Not many people even knew Natalie had a sister.

That made this remote cabin the perfect safe haven.

Which was exactly what Natalie needed right now.

A place where she could disappear. Where she could remain buried out of sight from the evil man who wanted nothing more than for her to die.

Natalie wasn't even sure why he was obsessed with her. Did this man want to silence her? Did he think she knew too much?

Or did he have a vendetta against her?

She still didn't know.

She only knew she wanted him to leave her alone.

But that wasn't going to happen. As soon as this man figured out where Natalie was hiding, she'd be dead. She was certain of it.

Her thoughts did nothing to ease her fears. But they were the truth.

She had the scars to prove it.

Her heart continued thrumming against her chest.

Even though she'd only been here for ten days, Natalie had grown to expect the quiet stillness. The cabin was surrounded by acres of uninhabited forest and seemingly endless mountains as the property backed up to a national park.

Maybe the wind had knocked something over outside. Or a raccoon was rifling through the trash can. Lexi had warned her about that.

She let out the breath she'd been holding.

That was probably it.

A raccoon.

Or was it a bear?

No, bears should be hibernating this time of year.

She glanced out the window but couldn't see anything. It was too dark out there.

At the thought, Natalie's gaze darted to the clock on the nightstand beside her.

It was 4:00 a.m.

She just wanted the sun to hurry up and rise. To expose anything lingering in the darkness.

Whatever that noise had been, it had pulled her out of a deep sleep.

Natalie sat still, listening.

Silence remained, almost mocking her as she gripped the quilt covering her.

"You're probably just imagining things," Natalie murmured to herself as she tried to get control of her thoughts.

That reassurance didn't stop her from reaching for the knife she kept in her nightstand.

She tucked the six-inch blade under her pillow before lying down again, reprimanding herself for overreacting. She pulled the quilt to her chin, wishing she could disappear beneath it and escape this entire situation.

What happened to the successful, confident person she'd once been? Would she ever regain her life? Her freedom?

Natalie wasn't sure. She hadn't known it was possible for fear to consume her like it did.

Her therapist had said she was having panic attacks.

Natalie didn't care what they were called.

She only knew the terror she felt when they came upon her.

No sooner had she nestled her head into the soft pillow did another noise thud outside.

It sounded like a heavy, booted footstep on the wooden porch that stretched in front of the cabin.

That was no raccoon.

Someone *was* out there.

He was out there.

Natalie was certain of it.

Trembling overtook her.

She couldn't just lie here. Couldn't just wait for this guy to break into the cabin and find her, to finish what he'd started.

That's when her thoughts turned to Lexi.

She should be home by now, tucked into bed after working the evening shift.

If anything happened to her sister because of her… Natalie couldn't finish the thought.

She should never have come here. Lexi had her fair share of problems already. She didn't need Natalie bringing hers.

Grabbing the knife again, Natalie slid out of bed. She pulled on some leggings and a sweatshirt before slipping on her boots. Since leaving the hospital after the attack, she always slept with them by her bed alongside a packed bag just in case she needed to run.

For the past several weeks, her whole life had revolved around her survival.

Natalie prayed she was overthinking the situation and that she'd never actually have to utilize the escape plan she often rehearsed in her mind.

But clearly she wasn't overthinking.

What she hadn't counted on was the real possibility of Lexi becoming collateral damage. In her mind, Natalie had run through survival scenarios, but only involving herself and the killer. Not Lexi.

She had to get her sister out of here before it was too late.

Knife in hand, she slid against the wall and as far away from the windows lining the porch as possible.

She'd leave the bag for now. If she had any hopes of escaping with her sister, she would need to be unencumbered. Nothing inside the bag was worth dying for.

Natalie crept toward her bedroom door. If she was going to make it, she'd have to slip into Lexi's room, wake her up and then take her through the living room, into the kitchen, and out the back door.

She had no time to waste.

But as Natalie took another step, a shadow crossed the window.

Her lungs froze.

The outline of a man appeared, first at one window, then another.

This guy was trying to peer inside, wasn't he?

Natalie sank into the shadows, praying he didn't see her.

She didn't dare make a sound.

But he must have seen her SUV outside. He had to know she was here.

Had he seen Lexi come home?

No telling how long he'd been out there watching the place.

Was he waiting her out?

Did he know she and Lexi had nowhere to go and no one around to help them? The nearest—and only—neighbor was a quarter mile away, and Lexi had warned her to stay away from the man. She'd said he was trouble.

More trouble was the last thing Natalie needed.

She remained frozen until the man finally stepped away and his silhouette disappeared. His boots again clunked against the rickety wood of the front porch.

Then she heard the doorknob rattle.

Her breath caught.

He was at her front door.

Trying to get inside.

He wasn't even trying to be quiet about it, as if he already knew he had the upper hand.

Despair threatened to overtake her.

Natalie couldn't let him get close enough to finish what he'd started.

She had to get Lexi and get out of here.

Her pulse continued to ramp up with every second that passed.

But she forced herself to move, to fight for her life.

She grabbed a jacket from behind her door and pulled it on. She always kept a flashlight in the pocket there. Then she grabbed her cell phone—which usually didn't even have service out here—stepped into the short hallway and headed toward Lexi's room.

"Lexi!" Natalie called in a hushed tone. "We have to go!"

Careful not to trip over the clothes strewn across Lexi's messy floor, she made her way to the bed and flipped on her flashlight.

She sucked in a breath.

Lexi's bed was empty.

Natalie whirled around. "Lexi!"

Next she checked the bathroom. It was also empty.

Lexi wasn't home, was she?

She didn't know whether to be relieved or more frightened.

But Natalie couldn't allow fear to immobilize her. She had to get out of here.

Now.

From where Natalie stood, she barely saw the outline of the man's head in the small glass pane atop the front door. A curtain covered it. He couldn't see inside.

But she'd seen enough.

The man rattled the door again, this time more insistently.

Then a thud sounded. Was he trying to kick in the door? It had a dead bolt, but she doubted the frame would withstand the pressure.

As panic raced through her veins, Natalie crept toward the back of the house.

She slipped through the kitchen to the back door.

Pausing to be sure the man was still at the front door, she listened.

When she heard the front doorknob rattle again, she lifted a prayer for courage and protection and darted outside toward the vast expanse of tree-dotted mountains surrounding her.

Suddenly, her seclusion felt like an enemy instead of a friend.

She flung herself down the wooden steps, cringing with each creak that sounded in the wood.

As soon as her feet hit the grass, she began sprinting, running as if fire chased her. She still gripped the knife, clutching it in her hand and praying she didn't stumble and cause her own demise.

Behind her, someone yelled, "Hey! Stop right there!"

The man.

He'd seen her.

Natalie fought through the panic and continued running toward the trees.

A few more steps and she'd be in the forest.

If she made it in time.

Because footsteps pounded behind her, destroying everything in their path and threatening to soon destroy her.

Andrew Moore held on to his dog's leash as the two of them took a nighttime walk.

It was the middle of the night, but Andrew was an insomniac. When Rambo—his three-year-old Newfoundland—had begun barking at him, he'd given up trying to sleep. The dog didn't usually do that unless he had a good reason, so Andrew had gotten dressed and headed out.

The nighttime air here in the Smoky Mountains was cool and crisp, as always in the winter. There was no snow right now, but only two weeks ago they'd gotten several inches.

He loved it out here. Loved the mountains. The hiking. The solitude. Out in these mountains, his biggest worries were bears, snakes, or overzealous tourists. This time of year, all three were scarce.

Being here beat his old life back in Nashville by far.

In Nashville, he'd worked his way up from a patrol officer to homicides. Rambo had faithfully been by his side for three years, and Andrew had often called the dog his right-hand man. Together, they'd solved uncountable crimes.

But the good the two of them had done together suddenly meant nothing—all because of lies someone had told about Andrew.

Lies that had demolished his reputation.

Rocky Cove, Tennessee, was the place where he'd come to recover after his life in Nashville had been upended. That was what Andrew told himself when he moved here. He just needed a fresh start.

He had enough money to sustain him for a couple more months until he could figure out his next plan of action. One thing was certain: from here on out, he wanted to do life alone.

He thought he'd had his future planned out with the woman of his dreams by his side.

But she'd stabbed him in the back.

The betrayal cut deep, and the wound was permanently embedded in his heart.

It was just as well. He had all he needed right here.

As Rambo sniffed around, a sound suddenly cut through the air.

It sounded like a man's voice calling out.

He squinted as his muscles tensed.

Only one person lived nearby—a woman named Lexi who had a cabin a quarter mile from his. As far as he knew, she lived there alone.

When Andrew had gone to introduce himself after she'd

moved in a month and a half ago, the thirty-something woman had been standoffish.

It had been more than being standoffish, however. The woman's eyes had been glazed, and he'd smelled the alcohol on her breath, and her speech had been slurred.

Not wanting to get involved, he hadn't gone back since.

But just last week, he'd noticed a woman driving an expensive SUV past his house. Since the road ended near his neighbor's cabin, the only person who normally came past his place was Lexi. If she had a boyfriend, he hadn't seen the guy.

So who had been yelling from that direction?

It certainly wasn't Lexi or the other woman.

The voice was too deep.

He hadn't seen the new woman bring anyone else over there either.

Andrew had seen her leave and return only one other time. From the glimpse he'd gotten of her, he'd guess she was probably in her late twenties or early thirties. She had dark hair that fell past her shoulders in waves, and she looked a lot like Lexi—only more civilized.

Either way, she didn't seem the type who'd want to live out in a place like this. Especially not with that fancy SUV she drove. Rather, he'd pictured her more as the urban type. With his cop's instincts, he usually had a good read on people.

Andrew would be lying if he said he wasn't curious about her—about both of the women, actually. But he'd minded his own business. He didn't want people to ask questions about him, so he didn't ask about others either. The law of reciprocity—only in a potentially negative sense, he supposed.

His muscles tensed as another shout reverberated through the woods. It sounded closer and had definitely come from a man.

His law enforcement instincts kicked into gear.

"Let's go make sure everything's okay," he told Rambo.

Rambo seemed to agree because the dog pulled him in the direction of the noise.

They cut through the patch of woods that separated the two properties.

A large plot of land stretched between them, all thick forest, dotted with large boulders and imposing rocks. Right now, since it was winter, the trees were barren and dry leaves covered most of the sloped ground. The skeletal branches made it easier to see, but the leaves made the forest floor slippery.

Andrew paused as he heard footsteps moving quickly in his direction.

Then he heard a cry. A woman's cry.

His lungs tightened.

Someone was running through these woods. In the dark.

Something was wrong. He was certain of it.

He picked up his pace as he headed toward his neighbor's cabin. He continued to weave between the trees, around rocks and through ravines.

As he got closer to the sounds, Rambo pulled harder on the leash.

He reached the top of a ridge, and a feminine figure appeared from around a boulder and collided with his chest.

Something flew from her hand.

A knife, he realized.

Andrew sucked in a breath.

The woman gasped as she looked up, her dark hair wild and covering half her face. Panicked eyes met his before she pushed herself away. She nearly toppled to the ground in the process.

Andrew caught her before she could fall. But as soon as he grasped her arm, she flinched. Even more panic seemed to set in.

She wrenched her arm out of his grasp and staggered backward.

This time, she did fall. She landed on her palms, but if she was hurt, she didn't let it faze her.

As her gaze landed on Rambo, she let out a strangled cry and scooted backward.

Once out of reach of the dog, she glanced behind her as if she expected someone to be there.

She kept glancing back and forth as if she was trapped.

Andrew peered into the darkness behind her.

No one was there.

He sucked in a breath before asking, "Are you okay?"

He studied the woman cautiously, unsure what she might do next. But he knew fear when he saw it.

This woman was terrified.

Andrew would need to proceed carefully. He didn't want to frighten her any more than she already was. Then there was that knife…thankfully, it had fallen out of her reach.

But he reminded himself that this woman could still be dangerous.

As Rambo barked and crept closer, the woman let out another gasp. Her eyes widened as she stared at the canine.

She scrambled back farther, her face turning sheer white.

She was terrified of dogs, wasn't she?

"Heel, boy," Andrew ordered. "Heel."

Rambo faithfully sat beside him, just as he'd been trained.

"He won't hurt you," Andrew assured her.

But the woman didn't seem any less afraid.

Instead, she rubbed her wrists, and Andrew wondered if she had a sprain.

As the woman glanced over her shoulder again, Andrew heard a stick crack in the distance.

She was being chased, wasn't she?

The man was after her.

That was why she'd had that knife.

Just then, Rambo growled.

The person who'd caused her to run must be close.

Andrew braced himself for whatever would happen next.

TWO

"It's going to be okay," the man in front of her muttered.

But nothing felt okay with Natalie. A killer was chasing her. Now she was stuck in the woods with a strange man and his vicious dog.

And her knife…where had it gone?

She'd dropped it, just like an airheaded heroine might in one of those scary movies.

That knife had been her one chance at defending herself…

The dog barked again.

With every *woof*, more breath left Natalie's lungs.

It was partially the fact that the dog was barking at something.

And partially the fact that he was a dog.

He seemed to listen to his owner, but still…what if his owner instructed him to do something deadly?

Every time he barked, she imagined what it would feel like for the canine's teeth to sink into her skin and rip her flesh from her body.

She wasn't sure what scared her more right now—the killer approaching from behind her, the man in front of her, or the dog barking at eye level to her.

But as she heard a crack in the distance, panic tried to claim her again.

Natalie forced in a deep breath as she tried to remain in control.

She couldn't fall apart right now.

She had to keep her wits about her.

A level head was her only chance of survival.

She looked up at the stranger staring at her as if she'd lost her mind.

But then the dog resumed barking ferociously.

"What is it, boy?" the man muttered.

Natalie glanced at the canine as it sat at attention, looking in the direction of her cabin. His fur stood up in a straight line down his back.

He knew someone was out there too, didn't he?

For a moment, she felt a fast bond with the dog.

Then she remembered how animals were unpredictable. How they could turn on people in an instant.

She stood, wiped the dirt from her tender palms and took a step back from the dog. Her trembling grew even stronger as the cold air seemed to sweep right through her clothing.

How was it possible that only a few months ago her life was going so smoothly? She had felt so confident and in control. In fact, others had told her she was someone people had admired and aspired to be like.

Had she become too arrogant? Too self-reliant? Was God allowing her to go through this as a matter of humbling her?

Maybe.

How the mighty had fallen. Wasn't that how the saying went?

Natalie was living that reality right now.

"Do you hear something, Rambo?" The man knelt beside his dog.

The canine began to pull him in the direction of the sound.

As he stood again and started to follow the dog's lead, Natalie tried to sink into the shadows. She didn't want to go with them. Didn't want to face that man.

But she didn't want to be left here in the woods alone either.

She glanced around, desperately searching for her knife.

But it was too dark.

She didn't see it.

"Wait…" She held up a hand before the man left. "Please, don't leave me out here alone."

The man paused and shook his head. "I wasn't planning on it."

Before they could speak any further, she heard something scampering.

Leaves crunched. Sticks cracked.

The man who'd been following her was running.

And he wasn't running toward them either. He was fleeing.

The realization brought her a significant amount of relief, which was immediately followed by another burst of anxiety.

What was she supposed to do now?

What if this guy went back to the cabin and waited for her there? Or what if he'd decided to hide out in the woods somewhere, anticipating he'd come across Natalie again whenever she finally headed home?

A shiver coursed through her.

She was far from being out of danger.

As goose bumps raced across her skin, she crossed her arms and rubbed them, desperate to calm herself.

Could she go into shock? She wasn't sure, but she didn't want to find out.

The man in front of her paused and turned to observe her a moment. His gaze was full of questions, yet it softened as he seemed to sense her distress.

"Do you want to tell me what's going on?" he asked.

Natalie licked her lips as his question hung in the air.

The truth was, she wasn't sure if she wanted to tell him or not.

It was a long, sordid story. She wished she could forget everything that'd happened back in Cincinnati.

But that wasn't possible.

Trouble had followed her here. She couldn't pretend this wasn't happening.

However, she had no idea if she could trust this guy, and opening up about her problems with a stranger made her feel entirely too vulnerable.

Natalie didn't see herself overcoming that any time soon.

It had been a long time since Andrew had seen a woman look so terrified.

He wasn't sure who'd been chasing her, but the woman was truly frightened.

He'd heard those footsteps in the distance.

Someone had clearly been out here.

In other circumstances, Andrew might have followed them.

But he sensed the woman shouldn't be left alone.

Until he knew more details, Andrew decided he would hold back.

His question still lingered in the air, and the woman stared at him. *Do you want to tell me what's going on?*

She licked her lips and met his gaze, as if she might answer. Then she looked away into the darkness and pressed her mouth shut again, as if uncertain.

Andrew had seen enough bad outcomes of domestic violence to suspect the nighttime intruder might be someone she knew. Maybe an abusive husband or boyfriend.

A stalker? Had she come here trying to get away from someone?

What he *did* know was the more he knew, the more he could help her.

He hadn't come here to immerse himself in anyone else's problems, but there was no way he could simply return to his cabin and leave this woman out here on her own.

"You don't have to tell me anything you don't want to," he finally said. "But at least let me and Rambo walk you back to your place."

Something close to relief seemed to seep through her at his words. Her shoulders softened as well as her gaze.

"I'd hate to bother you." Her voice trembled uncontrollably.

"It's not a bother. I offered." Andrew nodded in the direction she'd appeared from. "This way, I assume?"

She glanced around, as if uncertain. "I... I think that's right. Honestly, I just started running, and...now I'm all turned around."

"There aren't many homes around here. I'm pretty sure I know which way to head. Why don't you walk alongside me, just for safety reasons? The terrain is uneven out here."

She nodded, and Andrew waited for her to join him.

Rambo seemed to instinctively know which direction to lead them.

Andrew would guide the dog if necessary but, for now, he trusted the dog's intuition.

He wished he'd brought his gun with him. His cop instincts were on high alert. Even though he wasn't currently working, he knew when danger was close.

It definitely felt nearby right now.

The man who'd been chasing this woman could be hiding anywhere out here. Just because the guy had run didn't mean he couldn't have circled back around.

At that thought, the hair on Andrew's arms rose.

The person who'd spooked this woman…he was still close, wasn't he?

In fact, he could be watching them in the darkness right now.

Again, Andrew wished he had brought his gun along with him.

He'd always had it with him back in Nashville. But out here, he'd grown accustomed to leaving it in the cabin.

Rambo was a good backup, but Andrew would only turn Rambo loose as a last resort. The dog naturally had protective instincts. But he'd be no match against a gun.

He had brought some bear spray with him, which could work in a pinch. But the darkness wasn't his friend right now, and bear spray wouldn't help either if this guy had a gun.

As he and the woman reached a rocky portion of the mountain, Andrew extended his hand to help her.

She stared at his outstretched arm a moment before finally slipping her soft fingers into his.

Andrew helped her down the outcropping before they continued through the dark woods.

They didn't have much farther to go, but he refused to let down his guard.

Considering the way the woman's eyes kept darting around, she wasn't about to let down her guard either.

Andrew still sensed unseen eyes on him, and he didn't like it.

Had he left trouble in Nashville only to find it here?

"Do you want to tell me your name?" he finally asked.

The woman licked her lips. "Natalie."

"Natalie, I'm Andrew. I'm staying in the cabin just down the road. I'm assuming you're staying at the last cabin before the road ends?"

She nodded. "My sister's house, actually."

"Lexi is your sister?"

Her surprised gaze shot up to meet his. "Do you know Lexi?"

"I met her when she first moved here."

He didn't bother to mention that he hadn't been impressed by the woman.

He wondered if Natalie was anything like her.

His first instinct was no.

Natalie seemed astute and aware of her surroundings. Not glazed over like Lexi had been. But given the circumstances they were in right now, it was hard to say for sure how the two sisters differed.

Finally, he spotted a warm glow in the distance. "Did you leave a porch light on?"

Natalie seemed to think about it a moment before nodding.

"Yes. My sister wasn't home when I went to bed, so I left the light on for her." She suddenly stopped walking and breathlessly muttered, "Lexi."

Her face paled.

"What is it?" Andrew stopped beside her.

"She didn't come home. When the man showed up..." Natalie waved her hand. "I went to get Lexi out of there too as I left, but she wasn't there."

"Is that unusual?"

"She works as a waitress in Gatlinburg. Her restaurant doesn't close until one, and sometimes people stay late. So it's not unusual for her not to be home until two or two thirty."

He glanced at his watch. "It's getting close to 5:00 a.m."

Natalie began walking at a brisk pace. "Maybe she's back now."

She could be, but Andrew hadn't seen any headlights coming down the road as they'd trekked through the woods.

Who was the man chasing Natalie? Was he somehow connected with Lexi?

Andrew supposed those answers weren't any of his business.

He picked up his pace, determined to see Natalie back to the cabin safely. What happened from there, he didn't know.

But he could rest easy knowing he'd done what he'd been able to do to help her.

Just as the thought came to him, his gut told him that this wasn't over yet.

Finally, they reached the clearing, and the cabin came into view. Based on the way Natalie glanced at the gravel driveway and frowned, Lexi still wasn't home—her car wasn't there.

She was clearly worried about her sister.

Natalie turned to him. "Thank you. And again, I'm sorry that I… Wait. What were you doing out so early anyway?"

Although Andrew could go into details, and a part of him wouldn't mind having someone to talk to about the unfair circumstances that had upended his life, he would keep to his decision to live a solitary existence.

"Couldn't sleep," he answered simply.

Natalie tilted her head as if sensing there was more to his story, but if she was curious, she didn't ask.

Still, something in Andrew's gut told him not to leave. Not quite yet.

"Listen, I'd feel better if I checked out your place before I left," he said. "I know you don't know me. But whatever is going on has you shaken. I just want to make sure there's nothing to be concerned about here."

Just as before, his question hung in the air.

He waited with anticipation to see how Natalie would respond.

* * *

Natalie thought about Andrew's question.

Should she let this stranger inside the cabin? Could she trust him?

She wasn't sure, especially since he'd told her he lived in the cabin next door.

Lexi had warned her to stay away from the man, but her sister hadn't said why.

Then again, Lexi's opinions often didn't line up with Natalie's.

Natalie's gut indicated she could trust this guy.

But what if her intuition was wrong?

She sucked in a deep breath, inhaling the crisp, early-morning air and the scent of dried leaves and earth. She'd dealt with countless demanding executives in her career. She'd been known as being calm under pressure. Solid. Unbreakable.

She didn't feel that way anymore. But if this man wasn't safe, he'd had plenty of opportunities to hurt Natalie during their walk. Yet, he hadn't made any type of move.

He'd only been kind to her.

Maybe he really was one of the good guys.

"Okay," she finally croaked out. "You can check the place out. I'll wait on the porch while you do."

"Whatever makes you comfortable."

They walked to the front door, and Natalie let him inside. Just as she'd said, she waited outside, anticipation thrumming in her ears.

What if Andrew found someone hiding inside?

What if that man who'd been chasing her had fled back to the cabin and was now waiting for her?

The questions pressed on her until an ache formed in her head.

She'd come here to escape. To hide.

But what if hiding wasn't truly possible?

If that man had discovered her here, where would she go next? Going to Lexi's had been her backup plan. She didn't have another one.

But she'd had to run. Staying in Cincinnati wasn't safe.

She'd rented a friend's vacation home in Michigan for a while…until it became apparent the killer had found her again.

Coming to Lexi's was her last resort.

A snap sounded beside her, and she flinched, nearly jumping out of her skin.

But when she looked up, only Andrew stood in the doorway, his dog beside him.

She got her first real look at the man under the muted light of the porch.

He was tall with a five-o'clock shadow and light brown hair. His eyes were crystal blue and his build muscular.

A spark of attraction ran through her, which was the last thing Natalie needed right now. She forced her gaze away and looked at his dog instead.

The dog had dark, almost black fur and a thick build, almost like a Saint Bernard.

Though she was terrified of dogs, something about this one didn't seem as intimidating. His eyes were soulful, and his tongue hung from his mouth like he wanted to play a game of fetch.

"It looks clear to me," Andrew announced, pulling her from her thoughts.

Relief filled Natalie. "Thank you for checking things out."

"It's no problem. By chance, could the person who showed up here tonight be one of your sister's friends? Maybe a boyfriend who stopped by when he thought she'd be home from work?"

Natalie frowned as she thought about his question. "No, she would have told me she was expecting someone."

Lexi would have told her that, right?

Besides that, the guy would have knocked and not skulked around the cabin.

But her sister had problems of her own. In fact, Natalie suspected that Lexi might be doing some drugs on occasion.

Natalie had gone as far as searching the cabin, but she hadn't found any evidence.

She just knew that as sisters, she and Lexi were as opposite as they came. Though they looked so much alike that people at one time had mistaken them for twins, their personalities were night and day.

"Are you sure you're going to be okay here by yourself? I can follow you into town if you'd like and see if you can find a different place to stay until this passes over." Andrew stared at her, an earnest look in his gaze.

Was that what she should do? She knew she wouldn't feel any safer somewhere else, though. Right now, she felt as if her life dangled by a thread. Danger was around every corner, and her body seemed to be permanently poised for fight or flight.

"I think I'll just stay here," she finally said. "But your offer was kind. Thank you."

Andrew's gaze remained on her another moment.

She didn't know this man, but he was concerned about her, wasn't he?

She also realized that the concern in his gaze could grow to curiosity. And curiosity could lead to questions. And questions could lead to her demise.

Natalie couldn't let that happen.

She raised her chin, determined to be strong. "Thank you again for everything you did. I think I'll just lie down and see if I can get some rest until Lexi gets home."

He reached into his pocket and handed her a card. "If you need anything, this is how you can get in touch with me.

Don't hesitate, okay? Call 911 first, then call me. Because I'll get here sooner than they will."

She glanced down at his card and squinted. "You're a cop?"

Lexi hadn't told her that—probably because her sister hated cops after she'd had a few run-ins with the law.

But Andrew also hadn't told her. Why hadn't he? Didn't police officers automatically identify themselves as cops?

But he wasn't a cop here in this area. No, he was from Nashville.

So what was he doing here?

Natalie's curiosity spiked, but she shoved it down.

It really didn't matter what the answers were.

Just because he'd helped her out tonight didn't mean she'd become his responsibility.

With another lingering glance, Andrew stepped toward the woods with his dog. "Have a good night, Natalie."

"You too. Thank you again."

But as soon as Andrew and Rambo started walking away, Natalie instantly missed the man's presence.

THREE

Andrew's thoughts wouldn't stop racing as he waited to hear Natalie's door lock.

Once he knew she was safely inside, he stepped away from her cabin.

But he didn't hurry away.

There was something else he wanted to check.

"Come on, boy," he said to Rambo.

With his flashlight in hand, Andrew shone the beam onto the ground near the back steps.

Footprints. Just as he'd suspected. And those were definitely a man's footprints. They led from the back of Natalie's house to an old stack of wood behind the cabin.

From there, the prints led into the woods.

Someone *had* been following her, and he had a feeling Natalie had a good idea of who it was. This wasn't a simple misunderstanding no matter how Natalie might want to portray it.

Tension snaked up Andrew's spine at the thought of it.

He shone his light around in the woods again, looking for anything else out of place.

Or anyone who might be watching.

He still saw nothing.

But that didn't mean no one was out here.

He glanced back at Natalie's cabin. "What should we do, boy?"

His dog stared up at him.

Andrew frowned before letting out a sigh. The sunrise was due in another couple of hours. But he still hated to leave Natalie alone.

He didn't know her well enough to offer to stay. It was too cold outside for him to simply linger in the woods. Besides, that might freak her out even more.

For now, he needed to rest assured that the cabin was secure and that no one could get inside. Plus, Natalie had his phone number. From the time she contacted him, Andrew could hop in his truck and be here in less than five minutes.

He started back through the woods, his senses on full alert.

He'd grown up learning how to navigate the forest. His dad had taken him hunting and camping more times than he could count.

He practically felt at home between the trees.

But right now, the forest didn't feel welcoming.

No, he felt as if a predator lurked in the shadows. Even Rambo seemed to sense it. The dog's steps were tight, and he appeared on alert.

Andrew scanned everything again but saw no one.

As he continued to walk, he remembered the inside of Natalie's cabin.

One bedroom had been an absolute wreck. Clothes and shoes were everywhere. Each surface was littered with hair products and makeup. One whole wall had been plastered with pictures.

That had to be Lexi's room.

But the other bedroom was clean and neat with everything in its place.

He only assumed that was Natalie's.

Perhaps the sisters really *were* opposites.

Because he didn't have a good impression of Lexi. In fact, after the first time they met, he made a mental note to stay away from her.

She had a wild look in her eyes and hadn't made a secret of the fact that she didn't appreciate him stopping by to introduce himself.

On the other hand, Natalie had a way about her that seemed genuine. He could see her as warm and welcoming to her friends, yet with a healthy layer of caution to those she didn't know well.

Although he tried to stop thinking about Natalie, he couldn't.

What had brought her here? She didn't seem like the mountain cabin type. Not with her expensive-looking highlights and designer clothes.

Yes, he had noticed.

He'd been a detective for six years, so details were something he always paid careful attention to. It had become second nature to him.

A stick cracked in the distance, and Rambo's fur rose.

The dog let out a low growl.

Someone was still out there, weren't they?

He glanced around, looking for the source of the noise. But the darkness concealed it.

The next instant, something whizzed through the air.

A bullet, he realized.

Someone was shooting at him.

A distinctive popping noise echoed off the surrounding mountains.

Natalie froze as she paced her living room.

Had that been a...gunshot?

More fear shimmied up her spine.

That was exactly what it had sounded like.

Her heart beat harder.

What if the man who had tried to get into her house was waiting in the woods? What if he had somehow hurt the Good Samaritan who'd tried to help her tonight? Andrew and his dog, Rambo.

Her head began to spin, and she could hardly breathe at the thought of it.

But if this man was who she thought he was—and she was nearly certain he was—then he might see someone like Andrew as a threat. Someone who could stand in the way of his plan being exacted.

She'd known from the moment the man had broken into her house back in Cincinnati that nothing was going to stop him. He had intended on killing her that fateful night, but she'd survived. And now he wanted to finish what he had started.

She stared at the man's phone number in her hands. Should she call him?

If he was being shot at, then he certainly didn't need his phone to distract him. Or the sound of its ringing to draw attention to him depending on the circumstances.

She wanted to run outside. To find him. To help him.

Yet she felt frozen exactly where she was.

What if she just got in the way?

She pressed her eyes shut. *Dear Lord, what should I do?*

But she had no idea. Her courage seemed to disappear like the morning fog in the sun.

She couldn't just stand here. Especially not if this was her fault.

She glanced around the room, looking for something that might help her.

The previous owner of this cabin had left a wooden walking stick in the corner, and Lexi hadn't bothered to do anything with it. Natalie had picked it up once, and it was heavier than she'd thought it would be. She didn't have a gun—even though she had thought about buying one.

Too bad she'd lost that hunting knife.

She swallowed hard again as she imagined going up against a gunman with a walking stick.

She would be doomed from the start.

But she had to do something.

Her hands were trembling as she walked toward the door.

She had to go out into those woods again.

She had to help Andrew.

Because if something happened to him, she wasn't sure how she would live with herself.

Death seemed to surround her lately.

And she wasn't okay with that.

Andrew ducked behind a tree, pulling Rambo with him.

Just as he did, another bullet flew.

Whoever was out there meant business.

How much ammunition did this man have? A full round of ammunition would typically be fifteen bullets, depending on the gun model.

Could Andrew hide out here behind the tree for that long? How aggressive would this guy become? Would he move closer until Andrew had no choice but to either give himself up or run?

He wasn't accustomed to running. No, he usually faced danger head-on.

But he didn't like the fact that this guy had a weapon, and he didn't.

Back in Nashville, Andrew would have backup to call in. But out here, it was just him and Rambo.

Rambo whined beside him. The dog didn't like this any more than he did.

"It's okay, boy," Andrew whispered.

But as soon as the words left his mouth, another bullet cut through the air.

The bark on the tree next to him splintered.

Then several more rounds were fired.

But the trees around him took the bullets.

Rambo began to pant.

He was nervous, and Andrew couldn't blame the dog.

Andrew didn't like the odds either. This man was trigger-happy.

They couldn't just stand here. He had to do something before this guy found him and shot him point-blank.

When there was a break in the gunfire, Andrew darted to another tree, bending low to keep covered, Rambo at his side.

A rustling sound came from the right.

As he turned toward the noise, a shadow stepped out from behind a nearby tree.

It was the man. Dressed in black.

With a gun.

Before the man could pull the trigger, Andrew lunged at him and used his arm to shove the weapon out of the way.

The man's other fist connected with Andrew's jaw and pain shot through him.

The Glock discharged again, but the bullet went in the opposite direction.

The man grunted before diving toward him.

Andrew ducked, tossing the man over his shoulder.

He landed hard on the ground but righted himself again and turned toward Andrew.

The man still had the gun in his hand.

Rambo barked nonstop. The canine wanted to get at this guy. But Andrew knew this man wouldn't hesitate to shoot Rambo.

Before Andrew could tell the dog to stay back, the man raised his arm. Aimed his gun at Andrew's head.

With a deep, menacing growl, Rambo lunged at the man.

Then the man pulled the trigger.

FOUR

Silence followed the last sounds of gunfire.

Had Andrew been shot? Natalie wondered. Was the fight over?

Moments passed.

Natalie couldn't just stand here like a lump!

With the walking stick in hand, Natalie jerked open the door, ready to go out there and try to help.

But when she did, a man stood on the doorstep.

She swallowed a scream as he nearly tumbled inside.

Her eyes widened when she realized who it was.

"Andrew?" Something bad had happened to him. Blood ran down the side of his face. His breathing was labored, his gaze haggard.

She slipped an arm around him, sensing that he could use a hand, and led him inside.

"Rambo," Andrew called.

The dog loped inside, whining.

"I heard gunfire. A lot of it. What happened? Were you shot? Is Rambo okay? It looks like he's limping."

Andrew held up a hand as if to slow her rapid-fire questions. "Lock…the…door." He pointed at it.

Alarm raced through her. She rushed toward the door, slammed it shut and engaged all of the locks.

Her heart nearly pounded out of control as she turned

back to Andrew and studied him. "What happened? Are you okay?"

"He's still out there," he muttered. "He has a gun. I…"

Her heart pounded even harder if that was possible. "I heard the gunfire. Did he…shoot you?"

"He tried but didn't succeed. He just punched me. Got me in the jaw. We struggled for a while as I tried to get the gun away from him. He…he had me. I was done. Rambo lunged at him as he pulled the trigger, but he was out of bullets."

It sounded like Andrew had just barely evaded certain death. "What happened next?"

Part of Natalie wasn't sure she wanted details. Yet she had to know.

"Rambo knocked him down. The guy kicked Rambo off him then ran away. Rambo would have pursued him, but I didn't want my dog getting hurt so I called him off. I guess sometime in there, one of his paws was injured. But I checked. He's okay, maybe a little sore."

"I'm so sorry I got you into all this." Natalie lowered herself on the couch beside him.

"It's not your fault. This is on him."

She started to reach for the cut on his jaw, but she stopped herself as she realized she shouldn't touch it. "I'm sure my sister probably has a first aid kit around here somewhere."

"A wet paper towel and an ice pack is all I need."

Natalie stood and then glanced at Rambo. Gratitude for the dog spiraled through her, but she couldn't bring herself to pet him. Not yet. Maybe not ever.

"I hope he'll be okay," she said.

"He's been through much worse. He'll be fine."

That was a relief.

Quickly, she hurried into the kitchen and got him what he needed.

Then she rushed back to Andrew. She dabbed the napkin on the cut on his jaw, clearing away most of the blood before handing him the ice pack. "I hope this will help."

He placed it on his jaw. "Thank you."

Rambo was still panting heavily.

Natalie went back to the kitchen and filled a bowl with water for the dog. She set it in front of him before quickly backing up, afraid to get too close.

Then she skirted around the canine and went back to the couch.

Andrew's haggard gaze met hers. "Who was that man? Why is he after you?"

She licked her lips and swallowed hard. She hadn't wanted to tell him earlier. But after what had happened tonight and Andrew's involuntary involvement, how could she keep this to herself?

"I think he followed me here from Cincinnati," she said. "I don't know for sure, but it's the only thing that makes sense."

"Why would he follow you? Do you know who he is?"

Natalie shook her head. "I don't know his name. I only know he killed eight people in cold blood."

"What?" Andrew stilled. "How do you know this?"

"Because after he killed them, he tried to kill me. I got away, but he's determined to finish what he started."

"You said he killed eight people?" Surprise laced Andrew's voice. "Were they shot?"

"Yes. All of them."

"That sounds vaguely familiar."

"The murders were all over the news. The police have a lead, but I'm skeptical they're looking at the right guy. Even if they are, he's in the wind. It's been almost two months, and they haven't made an arrest."

Andrew studied her a moment. Natalie wanted to look away, but she didn't let herself. She needed to be strong.

"You were the only survivor?" he finally asked.

"Yes." Natalie's voice cracked as she said the word, and she rubbed her throat.

She'd tried to erase the memories of that horrible night from her mind, but it wasn't possible. They were still there whether she wanted them to be or not, forever etched into her memory.

Andrew was a cop. He certainly had some thoughts on this.

In fact, she could practically see him turning the facts over in his mind.

So she waited for what he had to say.

"This guy must have seen me as a threat and tried to get me out of the way," Andrew finally said.

His head was practically spinning.

He'd come here to get away from trouble, not to walk right into it. But it appeared that was what he'd done.

"I can only assume that's true." Natalie's voice sounded soft, yet scratchy with fear.

Andrew knew one thing for sure. This guy wasn't done yet. He would be back.

His actions tonight had proven that he was desperate. Probably single-minded. In fact, finishing what he'd started was probably the only thing this guy had been able to think about since his failed murder attempt.

But why? Why had he murdered those people to begin with? Something like that had to have been carefully planned out and executed.

He had so many questions, but Natalie didn't appear to be in the state to answer them. Her eyes were becoming glazed, and she continued to rub her jaw where a pink scar ran along her skin.

Whatever had happened to her, it hadn't been long enough for the scar to fade much.

"We should call the police," Andrew started.

"No!" Natalie seemed to realize how vehemently she'd said the word and her shoulders sank. "I mean, I don't want to get them involved. I really don't want people to know I'm here. I want to stay low-key, and if the media catches wind…"

"But this guy already knows you're here."

Natalie looked at him, yet only shrugged. "It's complicated."

"But the police might be able to help you."

She shook her head. "If you want to call them because of what happened to you, then that's fine. But right now, I just need some time alone to think."

Andrew couldn't just leave her here on her own. His parents had taught him to be a gentleman, and even though the concept of a man being protective over a woman was becoming old-fashioned and out of style in modern culture, he still believed that was the right thing to do.

No matter what, his stance on the issue wouldn't change. It was too ingrained in him.

Andrew glanced around and noted that this cabin wasn't nearly as secure as his own.

He looked at Natalie again, hoping he would be able to convince her to do what he was about to suggest.

"I want to take you with me. Away from this cabin." Andrew tried to keep his words gentle and not too forceful. He didn't want to scare her. And he *was* a stranger.

"But what about Lexi?" she asked. "What if she comes back and I'm not here?"

"Do you have any idea where she might be?"

"No. I have no idea. But it's not like I can just leave her a note and tell her where I'm going. The man could come back and see the note. Where is it you want me to go anyway?"

"Why don't you come to my cabin for now? I have some

security cameras hooked up. I'll see if they picked up on anything. Then when it's daylight, we can search the area. Maybe even call the police."

"I don't know." Her gaze skittered to the floor as if she was nervous.

"I know it seems unusual, and I know you don't know me. However, my impression is that you don't have anyone else in this area to turn to. Am I right?"

She glanced at her phone. "Aside from Lexi? No, I suppose I don't."

"Does she have a habit of not coming home sometimes?"

Natalie shrugged. "Not that I know of. I haven't been here with her that long, though. We were…slightly estranged before this."

"When did you say she usually gets home?"

"By two or two thirty at the latest. And it's already after five now. I'm really concerned about her. What if this guy got to her?"

Andrew didn't like the sound of that.

Natalie had a valid question—one he couldn't answer.

"I can help you try to get to the bottom of this. For now, what do you think about my idea?" He locked gazes with her.

The longer they stayed here, the more exposed he felt. At least at Andrew's place, he had installed new windows and doors. There were lots of safety latches. He'd set up several security cameras.

Plus, his gun was there.

Natalie glanced at the door and shivered. "I can't stand the thought of going back out there."

"I'll be with you."

"Why are you so willing to help me?" She stared at Andrew a moment as if trying to figure out his motives.

"Because it's the right thing to do. And it's who I am." The truth of his words reverberated within him.

If Andrew didn't serve and protect others, what would he do with himself?

But he couldn't think about his future in law enforcement now. That subject would have to wait.

"What do you say?" Andrew prompted, trying to keep his thoughts focused.

She finally nodded. "Okay. But if my sister comes back…"

"We should see her driving past on my security cameras, and you can call her. I have a landline, and I noticed you do too. Even without cell service you could talk to her if she's back at the house. She won't have any reason not to answer the phone. Unless…"

Natalie's eyes widened. "Unless what?"

On impulse, Andrew reached over and grabbed the phone off the kitchen counter.

His stomach sank.

It was as he'd feared.

The line had been cut.

Natalie felt her nerves thrumming inside her.

She had given her car keys to Andrew. She wasn't sure if that had been a good idea considering he'd just been hit in the face.

But he seemed more levelheaded and more capable of driving than she felt right now.

She was a nervous wreck inside.

Thankfully, Andrew had thought to check the phone line. Not that it made her feel any better knowing it had been cut.

But now Natalie knew she wouldn't be able to call Lexi if she came home.

A fresh wave of anxiety rolled over her.

Would she ever be free from this killer? Sometimes it didn't feel like it.

It had been two months, and he was still trying to get to her. If he was going to give up he would have by now.

Andrew didn't ask her permission to allow Rambo into her SUV. But of course, she couldn't say no. The dog had proven to be an asset. But her muscles were rigid as she was all too aware of the canine's presence.

She had halfway expected someone to jump out as soon as she walked outside to get to the SUV. Or to be hiding in the back seat. Or... Any number of scenarios raced through her mind.

But none of that had happened.

Maybe Andrew really had scared this guy off for tonight.

Because outside, it was quiet. Even Rambo didn't seem to sense that anything was amiss.

Natalie hoped that she was reading the dog correctly.

Fatigue weighed on her as Andrew started the SUV and backed out of the driveway.

The road leading to the house was long and lonely. Something about it creeped Natalie out every time she drove down it. It reminded her of a scary film she'd seen as a child about an old, abandoned house located down a desolate mountain road.

She'd only come here because she'd been desperate. She much preferred city life. It was all she had known since she had been a child.

Natalie already missed the convenience of coffee shops and grocery stores on every corner. She couldn't imagine living like this indefinitely.

She heard Rambo panting in the back seat and her muscles tightened even more.

The sound threatened to take her back in time, but she forced her thoughts to focus.

She couldn't let herself fall apart any more than she already had.

Andrew pulled out of the driveway and headed down the road. Natalie braced herself, still halfway expecting to see somebody run out in front of them and block the road.

Someone dressed in black. With a gun.

Someone wanting to kill her.

But there was no one.

Her imagination had taken on a life of its own since this all began, and not in a good way.

Finally, they pulled up to Andrew's cabin.

It was set off far from the road, so she'd never seen it. But the place was noticeably larger than her sister's and more well taken care of.

Landscaping surrounded the place, and the yard was immaculate. Andrew took pride in his home, that much was obvious.

Andrew instructed her to stay in the car while he and Rambo checked things out.

Natalie hadn't missed his authoritative cop voice as he'd spoken the words—as if he was automatically on duty when danger might be just around the corner. She appreciated the protective side of him. His willingness to take extra precautions.

Several moments later he reappeared and opened her door for her. She climbed out and Rambo greeted her, tail wagging.

His leg must be feeling better. His limp was gone as he sidled up next to her.

She tensed a moment, but then reminded herself the dog hadn't shown any aggression toward her. Not all dogs were mean. Those that were aggressive were often trained and nurtured to be that way.

Andrew quickly escorted her into the house. "Make yourself at home."

"Thank you."

The inside was as neat and tidy as the outside, and the place had a hominess about it. The scent of cedar and pine filled the place, bringing Natalie a brief moment of comfort.

This was a nice change from her sister's place. Lexi wasn't much of a housekeeper, and Natalie was constantly picking up after her. She didn't understand how Lexi could live like she did.

Natalie sank onto the brown leather couch as Andrew got his dog some water and then checked all the doors and windows to be sure they were locked.

She noticed that he picked up his gun from a drawer and slid it into his waistband. Normally, Natalie wasn't comfortable around guns, but in this case, she was glad he had one available.

As he added layers of kindling and larger wood pieces to the fireplace and started a fire, his confident movements and defined muscles were…impressive.

Natalie forced herself to look away.

Philip had also been impressive at first—until his true character emerged and he'd become a total disappointment.

The two of them had met at a fundraising gala and had hit it off right away. Philip, a financial advisor, had been handsome and charming. He'd swept Natalie off her feet with his fancy dates and wide smile.

The first few months they'd been together had been wonderful…until the rubber had hit the road, as the saying went.

It took time to get to know a person. To *really* get to know someone. To see past their words and focus on their actions. A lot could be told about someone by the way they acted in high-pressure situations.

Philip had failed at anything but the superficial.

Long-term with him had been destined for failure before their relationship had even taken off.

He'd taken one look at her in the hospital after she'd been left for dead, and he'd thought of every reason possible to leave. Her face and arms had been cut up and covered with bandages. Her entire body was swollen. She hadn't been able to talk.

The bottom line was that he wasn't cut out for anything less than a perfect life—or a perfect girlfriend. No doubt he'd feared Natalie would have scars—both physically and emotionally—that would hinder their perfect future together.

He'd insisted he wanted to focus more on his work and getting his career off the ground. But she knew the truth: she no longer met his expectations.

Natalie counted herself blessed. Being bound to a person with no integrity was the last thing she wanted, and thankfully she'd seen his true self before investing any more of her life in the guy.

She would be just fine on her own…if this killer would just go away.

When Andrew was done, he sat down on the opposite end of the couch and turned to her, bringing her from her thoughts.

She anticipated the questions that she knew were coming.

She couldn't even blame him for asking. Not in these circumstances. Not after everything he'd been through. He'd almost been killed because of her.

Her gaze traveled to his injury at the thought. His jaw was becoming more bruised as time went on. It looked painful, but he hadn't complained.

"Have you tried calling your sister again?" he started.

"Not since we met in the woods."

Just to be sure, Natalie tried dialing Lexi's number again. The call went straight to voice mail.

She looked at Andrew and shook her head. "I don't have a good feeling about this."

It wasn't like her sister not to answer.

Part of Natalie wanted to jump into her car and take off to Gatlinburg, which was about twenty minutes away. Maybe she could drive up and down the streets and spot Lexi.

But the chances seemed so unlikely.

Still, Natalie couldn't sit back and do nothing.

If she called the police, they'd probably tell her something about her sister needing to be missing for forty-eight hours.

"Do you have the number of any of her friends?" Andrew asked. "You could call them."

"I know there's a guy she's gone out with a few times, but she didn't tell me his name. As far as I know, she doesn't have any close friends. Sure, there are some people she parties with sometimes. But ever since I've been here, she hasn't brought them by, and I have no desire to get to know them, so I never asked. Maybe I should have."

"You couldn't have known all this would happen." Andrew stared at the crackling fire a moment before looking back at her. "Would you be comfortable with me driving you to Gatlinburg to look for her?"

Natalie sucked in a breath at his proposal—feeling a touch of both fear and hope. "You think it would do any good? I'd like to go do that…it just seems like the odds are against us finding her that way."

"Maybe we could find some people to talk to. People she works with would be a good place to start. What do you say?"

"You don't have to take me. But I could go. Should I drive into town now?"

The lines around his eyes tightened. "Considering what happened this morning, I don't think you should go alone. It's a long, lonely drive out of these mountains to get to Gatlinburg. I'd feel better if I went with you."

"Are you offering as a cop? Or a neighbor?"

"Does it matter?"

Natalie shifted, tucking a leg beneath her. "I suppose not."

"If it makes you feel better, I worked as a detective back in Nashville. But you probably already saw that on the business card I gave you."

"I did notice that." Her thoughts raced. "But you aren't a detective anymore?"

"Technically, I am. I'm still in law enforcement. But I've taken a leave of absence."

Why did his voice seem to harden as he said those words? Natalie wondered what had transpired to make him come to the decision.

Had he gotten into some sort of trouble?

She decided not to read too much into it. She had other more pressing matters to think about. But not for the first time, she found herself wondering what made Andrew tick.

"Okay… I mean, if you don't mind, I would appreciate that. Maybe I'm still shaken from the events from tonight. I'm just at a loss as to what to do. It's just not like my sister not to return home at some point after work or to call. The nights she's been out partying, she's always told me ahead of time."

"I understand." Andrew glanced at the time. "I'd suggest we wait until a little later to head out. Everything is going to be closed right now, and it's still dark outside. In the meantime, how about if we check out the security camera footage?"

FIVE

A few moments later Andrew and Natalie sat at his computer.

He had a security camera at the entrance of his driveway that recorded everyone who came and went down the road.

Normally, the only people who came down this road were him, Lexi, the mailman and occasionally a delivery driver.

Andrew wanted to see if anyone else had gone by tonight.

He rewound his security footage by four hours and began to scroll. Natalie sat beside him, not saying a word, only watching.

After several minutes, he sighed.

"There's nothing," he muttered.

"So how did that man get to my sister's cabin?"

"That's a great question." Andrew rubbed his throbbing jaw. "Maybe he parked farther up the road and hiked in. But it doesn't seem like the best option."

"I guess it's possible…" But her tone made it clear she thought it was unlikely also.

It was dark outside, so there was a chance that Andrew's security camera wouldn't have picked up on a darkly clad figure trekking through the woods.

But somehow, that scenario didn't sit right with him.

If someone wanted to catch either Natalie or Lexi by surprise, he would likely want a vehicle closer in order to have a faster getaway after he'd done whatever he'd planned on doing.

Andrew wasn't sure exactly what that was, but he knew it hadn't been anything good.

Hiking trails were all over this area, but the closest major one was about a mile away. From the trailhead, someone would need to hike at least five miles to get to the area behind their houses.

So much about this whole scenario didn't make sense.

Andrew didn't know what he was getting himself into.

He probably shouldn't have offered to bring Natalie here. Part of his goal while living here was to not become involved with anybody or anything.

Yet here he was getting involved.

But how could he ignore someone who was in need?

Andrew knew the answer to that question.

He couldn't.

He'd heard the desperation in Natalie's voice, and he had no choice except to help her.

He'd come here to get away, heal and relax after the fiasco with his fiancée back in Nashville. He needed to figure out what his future might look like.

Andrew still wasn't sure.

But he wasn't interested in pretending to have his entire future figured out—nor was he looking for another romantic relationship.

No, for now it was just him and Rambo.

He glanced at his dog as the canine headed toward him, hoping for another head rub.

Andrew gladly obliged.

He glanced at the time again.

It had been an hour.

By the time they got cleaned up, it would be time for them to leave.

He prayed Natalie found the answers she was seeking.

He knew she had a problem with dogs, but he hoped she didn't mind if he brought Rambo along. Rambo could prove to be very helpful. Besides, these days, Andrew rarely went anywhere without him. That dog was his sidekick. They were a package deal.

As Natalie stepped out from the spare bedroom, Andrew sucked in a breath at the sight of her.

She'd cleaned up nicely.

Her dark hair was now in a tight ponytail. She wore a fuchsia-colored sweater and black skinny jeans along with her boots. Plus she'd pulled on a black coat along with a colorful striped scarf.

He'd noticed that Natalie was pretty before. But he'd had other things on his mind.

Seeing her now made him feel a rush of attraction—a rush of attraction he hadn't been expecting.

He swallowed hard and pushed his feelings down. "Are you ready?"

"Yes." She nodded quickly. "Thank you again."

He stepped outside, opened the door to his Bronco and waited for Natalie to climb in. Next, he let Rambo hop into the back seat.

A few minutes later, they were on the road.

It was now getting close to 7:00 a.m. The sun would be rising soon.

"Nice ride," she muttered as she glanced around the vehicle.

"Thanks. I fixed her up in my free time." He drove an old 1985 Ford Bronco. He'd restored it and worked on the engine before finally painting it sky blue—its original color.

"A man of many talents, I see."

He shrugged. "I don't know about that. But it was fun to work on."

Natalie glanced in the back seat.

"Tell me about Rambo." Her voice trembled as she said the words, but she swallowed hard as if pushing down her fear. "He seems to listen to you really well."

"He's trained to listen to my commands. Rambo is a search and rescue dog."

His statement seemed to capture her attention. "Is that like a police dog?"

"That's right. I've had him since he was ten weeks old."

"Does he live with you just like a regular pet would?"

"He does. He's like family. He's a smart boy and can do whatever I ask."

"Like what?"

"He can do all the commands I've taught him for search and rescue. But I don't want him to get bored so I'm always teaching him new things. I've been working on 'tidy up' lately."

She raised her eyebrows. "Tidy up?"

"He puts all his toys away."

"Impressive. What else can he do?"

"He can turn off the light, he can lower his head to 'pray,' and he can dance." He rubbed Rambo's head. "I rarely go anywhere without him. He was always with me on the job back in Nashville. Oh, and he can open doors too."

"What? How?"

"He taught himself that one. I left him alone at home one day in the spare bedroom, and he decided he wanted to get out and explore the house. That's when I realized he could act like Houdini and escape."

"I didn't even know dogs could use their paws like that.

I've seen cats do it, but dogs? That's fascinating. Did you guys solve any big cases together?"

"As a matter of fact, Rambo has helped find a few missing hikers, a person who was abducted, and two elderly people with dementia who wandered off."

"Impressive."

Andrew stole a glance at her. "I take it you don't like dogs?"

"I had a run-in with one once." Natalie touched the scar on her jaw.

He wanted to ask more questions, but he didn't feel it was his place.

Instead they fell into a comfortable silence the rest of the way.

Once they reached Gatlinburg, Andrew asked, "What do you say we start with the place Lexi works at?"

"That makes sense." Natalie told him the name of the restaurant.

A few minutes later, they pulled up in front of the Alpine Bistro and Barbecue.

As he parked his Bronco, Andrew prayed that Natalie would get some of the answers she was seeking.

Natalie stared at the restaurant.

Though "Bistro" was in the name and made her think of something small and quaint, the building in front of her looked like an oversize log cabin. The restaurant was nestled far enough away from the strip that the establishment had its own parking area. Lexi had told her that in the evenings, a parking attendant had to make sure only patrons parked there.

The scent of roasted pig, hickory wood chips, and various spices wafted through the air, making Natalie's stomach grumble.

"How long has Lexi worked here?" Andrew stared at the building also.

"About a month. Lexi tends to skip from job to job." Her sister had always been like that, ever since they were teens.

But when Lexi had gotten in with the wrong crowd during high school, her life had really gone in a different direction. It had all happened after their parents had divorced. Lexi had gone with their mother while Natalie stayed with their dad.

Their parenting styles had been vastly different, and Lexi and Mom had become more like friends with no real boundaries in place. Her father, on the other hand, had remained strict and had taught Natalie how to live with integrity.

He'd died last year after having a heart attack, and Natalie still missed him every day.

Natalie had tried to help Lexi, but her sister wouldn't listen. Instead, Lexi had begun to resent Natalie's interference, and eventually, Natalie simply had to take a step back. She couldn't force Lexi to make good decisions. She couldn't compel her sister to change. That had to be Lexi's own choice.

A tremble of nerves rippled through Natalie as she grabbed the door handle.

She stepped out into the mostly empty parking area. Andrew and Rambo climbed out behind her, and they all stood a moment studying the restaurant.

Coming here looking for answers was a long shot. Even though some staff would be here preparing for the lunch crowd, most likely it was a different set of employees than those who'd been here last night.

But at least coming here and asking questions would allow Natalie to do something. It beat sitting in her cabin overthinking things.

"Where do the employees usually park?" Andrew asked.

"I only came here with Lexi once. There are a few spaces behind the building, and I think that's where the general manager likes for them to park if possible."

"Let's see if her car is here then."

They started around the building, and as soon as they rounded the corner, Natalie stopped and pointed to a beat-up gray sedan. "That's it. Lexi's car."

Natalie's heart thrummed inside her.

She wasn't sure if seeing the vehicle made her feel better or worse.

As Andrew began walking toward it, Natalie quickly caught up.

She dreaded what she might find inside.

What if it was bad news? A confirmation of her worst fears?

Natalie forced herself to look anyway. There were some things Andrew wouldn't be able to identify as being out of place.

But Natalie could.

Using the hem of her shirt, she tried to open the door handle.

"Smart thinking," Andrew muttered. "Just in case there are prints there."

Something about his affirmation brought Natalie a touch of comfort.

But the doors were locked.

She bit back a frown. "That didn't work."

Instead, she cupped her hands around her eyes and peered inside the windows. She hoped to see something in the car's interior that might give her a clue about what had happened.

She sucked in a breath.

The seats were shredded.

"Why would someone do that?" she muttered.

Andrew glanced inside also and frowned. "That's a good question. I take it her seats weren't like that earlier?"

Had they been?

Natalie didn't know for sure. She didn't make it a habit to look inside her sister's car.

The two hadn't gone anywhere in the vehicle since Natalie arrived. The one time Natalie had gone to eat with her at the restaurant, Natalie had insisted on driving. Her vehicle was the more reliable of the two.

"I don't think so," Natalie finally answered.

"There's no blood," Andrew said. "That's a good sign. I still wonder if maybe Lexi just went home with a friend."

"I wish I could believe that, but it doesn't explain why she's not answering her phone." Natalie frowned.

"Maybe it died."

"Then why wouldn't she borrow someone else's phone to let me know?"

Andrew stared at her a moment, and she knew exactly what he was thinking.

If Lexi had gone home with someone and gotten high, then calling Natalie would be the last thing she'd think about.

Unfortunately, that scenario was a real possibility. Natalie didn't want to admit it, but she knew it was true.

At the end of the day, this all might be chalked up to Lexi's bad decisions.

Natalie had been there and done that before with her sister.

Part of her hoped that was the case now. She'd rather be mad at her sister for being irresponsible than face a situation where something bad had happened to her.

Andrew shifted toward her again, and Natalie knew that he was about to dismiss all of this and suggest that they go back to their cabins.

She couldn't blame him.

But before he said anything, the back door to the restaurant opened.

Dylan Murphy stepped out.

Dylan...a guy that Lexi said was one of her new friends. He was a cook here, and he usually worked the late shift with her.

Which was why Natalie was surprised to see him here in the morning.

But she wasn't complaining—because maybe he had some answers for her.

SIX

Andrew watched as the guy stepped from the building and spotted them. The man tensed a moment before his shoulders softened in recognition.

Natalie waved and called him over. He held something in his hand—it appeared to be a paycheck. It was the fifteenth of the month, so that would make sense.

The guy was probably in his early thirties, with spiky hair and earrings. He wore a tight black shirt and looked like he hadn't shaved yet for the day...probably on purpose if Andrew had to guess.

"You're Lexi's sister, right?" He looked at Natalie as he stepped closer.

"That's right," she said. "We met once when Lexi brought me here to eat. I'm Natalie, and this is my neighbor Andrew."

Andrew nodded at the man.

"What are you guys doing out here?" His gaze flickered to Lexi's car in the distance.

"My sister didn't come home last night, and I'm worried. When did you see her last?"

"When did I see Lexi?" He ran a hand through his hair and looked off at the mountains in the distance. "I left here about 2:00 a.m. last night. I'm nearly certain she left at one thirty. She stayed late to help us clean up. It was a busy night, and we had some customers that just didn't want to leave."

Andrew shifted as he tried to form a timeline in his mind. "How did she seem when she left?"

Dylan thought about it another moment before shrugging again. "Seemed fine to me. Like the normal Lexi."

"Was there anyone in the restaurant who paid special attention to her?" Andrew continued.

"You know Lexi…she always gets attention." Dylan let out a little laugh. "She's a real head turner. I'm sure there were guys flirting with her, but nobody that set off any alarms in my head." He paused and placed his hands on his hips. "You guys are really worried, aren't you?"

"It's not like her not to call," Natalie said.

"That doesn't sound like the girl I know." He let out another chuckle. "The Lexi I know thinks mostly about herself and nobody else."

Natalie frowned but didn't deny his words.

"I mean, I don't want to think that anything happened to her," Dylan continued. "But my guess is that she met some guy here and went home with him. That may not be what you want to hear. But that's the most likely truth."

Andrew glanced at Natalie and saw the frown tugging at her lips. She clearly didn't approve of what he had said.

"I'm going to need to talk to somebody else about this," Andrew said. "Is there a manager inside?"

"Yeah, but it's the day shift manager. You want to talk to Frank. He was the manager on duty last night. I can probably get his info for you. But I need to run it past management first."

"We'll wait," Andrew said.

"No problem."

As Dylan disappeared inside, Natalie wandered back over to Lexi's car.

Andrew watched as she inspected it. Walked around the entire car.

Watched as she knelt on the ground and peered under it.

That's when he heard a gasp.

His heart rate quickened.

What exactly had she discovered?

He rushed toward Natalie, Rambo beside him.

He feared the worst—though he didn't see any signs of trouble.

"Natalie?" Andrew called before kneeling on the ground beside her.

He peered under the car and saw exactly what had upset Natalie.

He took a tissue from his pocket and reached underneath to grab the object left there.

A cell phone with a smashed screen.

"This is Lexi's?" He glanced at Natalie, who looked pale and ashen.

She nodded. "Yes. No wonder she hasn't been answering."

Andrew touched her shoulder.

She flinched and jerked her gaze toward him.

Her limbs began to tremble again.

Andrew raised his hands, silently letting her know he wouldn't touch her again. He hadn't meant to shake her up. He hadn't expected her to be so jumpy either.

As her gaze remained on him, he saw the questions and uncertainty there.

But mostly, Andrew saw fear.

He wanted to help Natalie, to bring her out of her state of shock.

Yet he didn't dare touch her again.

Before he could ask any more questions, footsteps sounded behind them, and he spun to see who was approaching.

* * *

Natalie turned at the sound of footsteps.

A man with a name tag pinned to his shirt stood there—one reading "Jim Sullivan, Manager."

She released her breath.

There was nothing to be concerned about. Not about this situation, at least.

Natalie tried to pull herself together, but the task felt impossible.

Especially when she considered Lexi's smashed cell phone.

Someone had left it there on purpose.

He'd wanted her to have this exact reaction—fear.

It had worked.

The man was here. He'd found her.

She'd suspected as much before.

But now she was certain.

"I'm Jim, one of the managers here. Dylan tells me you have some questions." The man was in his forties with dark hair and a plump build. He looked both curious and cautious as he shifted in front of them.

Andrew began explaining that he needed to speak with some more staff members, and he flashed a badge.

Sure, it was a Nashville PD badge, but he was still law enforcement.

However, Natalie wasn't sure if that made her feel better or worse.

Lexi had always told her to stay away from cops. But she knew why her sister had said that.

Lexi had too many run-ins with the law. Her sister didn't trust any law enforcement because of that. But most of the predicaments her sister had gotten herself into were trouble of her own making.

That's why Natalie'd had so many reservations about coming here. She didn't want to get caught up in Lexi's problems. She'd learned long ago that trying to convince Lexi to turn her life around wouldn't work.

Lexi had to decide that for herself.

This hadn't been the first place Natalie had come. No, this was her last resort.

First, she'd escaped to Michigan.

When the man had found her there, she'd run again.

Coming here, she'd double-backed on many different roads to make sure she wasn't being followed.

But somehow, the man had found her *again*.

Natalie wasn't much for posting her personal life on social media, but she knew with the facial recognition software available these days, if Lexi posted a photo of the two of them together, someone with computer knowledge could put the pieces together.

Was it even possible to disappear anymore? To really go off the grid?

She was beginning to think it wasn't.

She sighed. Before all this happened, figuring out how best to disappear hadn't even been on her radar.

She tried not to be too hard on herself. Her specialty was working in advertising. Not hiding.

"Did you see Lexi here yesterday?" Andrew asked Jim, bringing Natalie's thoughts back to the moment.

"Briefly. I left just about the time she got here."

"Did anything seem off about her?"

Jim shook his head. "Not that I noticed. She seemed like her normal self. Nothing was out of the ordinary."

"Did you see anybody unusual hanging around outside of the building yesterday?" Andrew continued.

Jim seemed to think about it a moment before running a hand over his face and sighing. "I did see a guy hanging out back here when I took out the trash. He was standing near the dumpsters, pacing. He seemed preoccupied, but friendly enough. I didn't really think a lot about it because sometimes we get some strange characters passing through here."

"What happened?" Andrew asked. "Did he say anything?"

"He didn't talk to me. When he saw me, he just nodded and then meandered off. He was carrying a backpack, so I assumed he was just passing through. I figured no harm, no foul. I went on with the rest of my day."

"What did he look like?" Andrew shoved Lexi's broken cell phone into his pocket. "Do you think you could ID him if you saw him again?"

Natalie froze, hardly able to breathe as she waited for his answer.

He grimaced. "I don't know if I could pick the guy out of a lineup if that's what you're asking. I wasn't paying that much attention, but he was probably medium height and build. He wore all black clothing—including a drawstring hoodie and a black baseball cap." He shook his head. "I wish I could give you more, but I can't. I'm sorry."

"Did he have any tattoos that you noticed?"

"No, man. None on his hands or neck or anything."

"Okay. I also need to speak with the manager working last night." Andrew absently patted Rambo's head. "How can I contact that person?"

Rambo shifted, his tag jingling. Just the sound of it made goose bumps rise on her arms.

Would she ever get over her fear of dogs? It didn't seem so. She had every right to want to stay away from them, but she didn't want to live the rest of her life terrified of what a dog could do to her.

"Frank was working last night." Jim patted his pockets. "I think I have his number here on me. We just got these new business cards, so I've been handing them out to people, hoping they'll leave them lying around. You know, for advertising."

Natalie could give Jim some pointers on how to advertise a restaurant, and leaving things up to chance wasn't on her list. But she didn't say anything. That's not even remotely why she was here.

Finally, Jim found a card in his shirt pocket.

"Ah, here it is." He handed it to Andrew. "This is Frank's contact information. If I were you, I'd wait until after ten to call him. He worked late, and he likes to sleep in. He'll be much more likely to answer any questions for you after he's gotten at least six hours of shuteye."

"Got it." Andrew glanced at the card before storing it in his pocket.

Natalie checked the time on her phone. It was almost eight, so they still had a little time to wait until they could call this Frank guy.

What would they do in the meantime?

A slight breeze picked up, chilling Natalie as she glanced around the parking lot.

Was the guy who had been lingering back here connected with the fiasco back in her life in Cincinnati? What if he was the man who had tried to get into her house last night? Who had chased her through the woods? What if he was here right now and watching her?

Even worse…what if he'd done something to Lexi?

SEVEN

Andrew turned back to Natalie again. "Listen, we have some time to kill before we can call this guy. Why don't we grab some breakfast? It'll give us a chance to talk and to formulate a plan as to what we want to do next. Alpine is lunch and dinner only, but there are some other places around here."

Her shoulders softened and air left her lungs as visible relief washed over her. "Thanks for sticking with me on this. Even though you're under no obligation to..."

"It's no problem." He shrugged.

But he did appreciate the fact she was thankful for his help. But most of all, he was thankful he'd been there last night to run into her in the woods. Where would she be if he hadn't been?

Andrew didn't want to think that man would have caught up to her, but chances were good he would have.

She'd been unarmed. Basically defenseless.

She might not have made it through the night.

"Breakfast sounds good. What about your dog? You can't take him inside a restaurant, can you?" She glanced at Rambo, her face turning pale again.

She truly was terrified of dogs. But Andrew had to admire her resolve to push through her fears. Some people wouldn't be that strong or willing to be so obviously un-comfortable.

"There are a couple of restaurants around here where dogs are allowed. The ones with the heated outdoor patios. In fact, I know of just the place we can try. I think you'll really like it."

"Okay, I'm up for trying new things."

Another thing Andrew liked about her. She seemed to know what she was and wasn't willing to do. He had no doubt that Natalie could stand her ground in high-pressure situations.

Like the one she found herself in right now.

She was being proactive. Looking for a way to solve her problems, not whining about them or feeling sorry for herself.

No, she was facing her challenges head-on. He admired that about her.

"If it's okay, we should walk to the restaurant," Andrew said. "Parking around Gatlinburg can be tricky. Even if you're good at parallel parking, the spaces are limited on the streets. Besides, it's not too far."

"Walking sounds great."

They began strolling from the parking lot toward the sidewalk in the distance. The morning chill was already beginning to ease up as the air temperature rose to a more comfortable level.

As a few moments of silence fell, Andrew decided to strike up casual conversation. Maybe they could both use a moment of normalcy in this otherwise stressful situation.

"Do you come to the Smoky Mountains often?" he asked.

"I wouldn't say often. I've been here a few times. My parents brought my sister and I here on a couple of va-cations when we were younger. I always thought it was fun—especially doing the mountain coasters and exploring the shops. There always seems to be something new to see and do. Plus, eating some homemade fudge is a must."

"Can't go wrong with fudge. What else do you like to do here? Or what would you like to do here in different circumstances?"

"Well…" Natalie shrugged. "I enjoy people watching. I like finding a bench and sitting for a while, wondering what goes on in people's lives. What brought them here. What the future holds for them."

"So you're more of a people person than a nature enthusiast?"

"Don't get me wrong, I enjoy being outdoors as well. It's just always fascinated me, learning about other people. What makes them tick." She glanced up at Andrew, a sheepish look in her gaze. "I'm rambling, aren't I?"

"Not at all. How about hiking?"

"We did some hiking too. I think I'd probably appreciate hiking more now as an adult than I did as a kid. Back then, I was more of the bookish type. I suppose I still am." A frown crossed her features. "Well, at least I am when things are normal. I…haven't been able to concentrate on reading lately. So much has been on my mind."

"That's understandable."

They walked a few more minutes before Andrew stopped in front of a place named Mountaintop Pancakes. "Here we are."

The restaurant was designed to look like a place that might be found in the Swiss Alps, with its stucco siding and decorative wood framing.

"It looks quaint." Natalie looked over the place.

"Best pancakes in the area," he told her.

"Then I'll have to try some. I'm getting hungry."

Andrew stepped inside and talked to the hostess, who made over Rambo as if she'd gladly take him off Andrew's hands if he'd let her.

Several minutes later, Andrew, Natalie and Rambo were all seated on the outdoor patio with both a pergola and a heater overhead. Even though it was in the forties, it wasn't windy, and the overhead heater was surprisingly warm.

Natalie opened a menu and stared at it. "Anything you recommend? Or just the pancakes?"

"My favorite is the Smoky Mountain special. It's fantastic, and you won't be disappointed. It's got a little bit of everything, and their eggs are fresh from the farm."

She closed the menu. "Then that's what I'll have."

A few minutes later, they'd ordered, and their menus had been taken away, replaced with steaming cups of coffee. But first, Natalie had double-checked with the waitress about the use of peanuts in the restaurant.

The waitress assured her the meal she'd ordered would be safe for her to eat, and she would alert the kitchen staff about her allergy.

"You're allergic to peanuts?" Andrew asked when the waitress had left.

Natalie nodded. "Ever since I was a kid. I always hoped I'd outgrow it, but I haven't."

"That must be tough to deal with."

"As an adult, it's much easier. As a child, my mom was a nervous wreck whenever we had a social at school or I was invited to a party."

"I can imagine."

"She even had allergy cards printed out, so I could give them to kids' moms when I went to their houses for playdates."

"You must have had a bad reaction at some point."

"I did. It took three trips to the hospital before we narrowed the allergy down. At first, we weren't sure what was causing the issue."

"That's a scary thing for a kid to deal with."

"It was. It still is. But I have an EpiPen in case I ever

need it. I'm thankful that medicine exists to help counteract the effects. I just always have to remember to keep it with me."

After a few moments of quiet, Andrew leaned toward her, knowing there were things they needed to talk about.

"Listen, Natalie. I don't mind helping you," he started. "Not at all. But I'm going to need to know more before diving any deeper into this. I'm not sure exactly what I'm getting myself into, but there's clearly more to the story. If I'm putting myself on the line, then I need to know everything."

Natalie's throat burned at his statement. She'd known his inquiries would come. And it wasn't fair to him to keep him in the dark.

Still, she didn't like talking about what'd happened.

She leaned back in her seat, glancing at people as they walked past on the sidewalk. The area wasn't too busy this time of year, but there were still plenty of people passing by.

Before Natalie realized what she was doing, she caught herself searching the landscape for a man dressed in black.

"Natalie?" Andrew's voice brought her gaze back to his.

She licked her lips as she contemplated what to say. "The truth is, I'm an advertising executive from Cincinnati. Not to brag, but I'm good at my job, and I've had some high-profile clients over the years. I even had a waiting list of people who wanted to hire me, and that allowed me to be picky about who I took on."

"It's nice to be in that position."

"Usually," she told him. "Every once in a while, someone will get upset with me. Like the guy who did a startup of a company called Sent Scents that sends different aromas to people meant to stir memories of better times. The guy was a tech genius, apparently, but he wanted to give up that career for this new venture."

"Sounds interesting. Smells do have a strong link to memory. I learned that when I went through K9 training."

"It was an interesting concept. But the advertising dollars he'd need to launch that?" Natalie shrugged. "Unfortunately, he couldn't afford me. He didn't take the news well. In fact, security had to escort him out of the building."

"It sounds like he was very passionate about his idea."

"To say the least."

Natalie paused and took a sip of her coffee so she could compose herself.

She took in a deep breath, then continued. "Anyway, a few months ago, I took on a new client, Drexel—a Fortune 500 company. Before my team and I launched the campaign, some of the executives from Drexel were planning a dinner party, and they invited me to come. Unfortunately, I got held up in traffic on the way there, and I was about ten minutes late arriving. Maybe I shouldn't say 'unfortunately.' Being late to the party saved my life."

Andrew squinted. "What do you mean?"

"When I got to the house I rang the doorbell, but no one answered. There were several cars in the circular driveway, so I knew I had the right address. I tried the doorknob and found the door wasn't even latched shut. It swung open and I stepped inside… I saw the blood first. Then…the bodies. Everyone inside the house was dead. They'd been shot."

Andrew's eyes widened. "That must have been quite a shock."

She rubbed her throat again. "It was. I just assumed that whoever had done it was long gone. But as I grabbed my phone to call the police, a man dressed in all black stepped from a room off the main entrance. He had a massive dog with him. It growled at me, baring its teeth as it pulled against the leash. The man moved in front of the door and blocked the way out. I didn't stand a chance of escaping that way. Then the man…raised his gun at me, and I knew for sure he was going to shoot."

"How did you manage to get away?" Andrew stared at her, patiently waiting for her to continue.

She gathered herself before finishing. "Thankfully, I came to my senses and ducked out of the way just as he pulled the trigger. The bullet just barely missed me, and I took off in a run—and I kept running. I wasn't halfway thinking so I didn't really know what I was going to do. I just knew I had to keep moving."

"Sounds like textbook fight-or-flight. It makes sense."

"The next minute, I felt something on my heels. The man had let his dog off the leash and it—a German shepherd—chased me. Tackled me to the ground. I thought I was going to die. I tried to push it away, but it just kept coming at me. Biting. Tearing into my skin."

Natalie shivered as she relived the terrifying moments.

A few deep breaths later, she continued. "I think at some point I must have passed out. In fact, the man thought I was dead. I'm nearly certain that's the only reason he called his dog off and left me there. The next thing I remembered was a police officer standing over me and trying to wake me up. I'd lost a lot of blood at that point and…well, I think you get the gist of it."

"I'm so sorry that happened to you. No wonder you're frightened of dogs." Andrew reached down and rubbed Rambo's head. "They're not all bad."

"I know. But my attack…it was horrible." Natalie touched the scar on her jaw. "This is just one of the permanent reminders I have. My legs and part of my arm took the worst of it."

Andrew frowned again. "Was this guy ever caught?"

"No. I think he's the one who was at the cabin last night. The man who chased me through the woods."

"Why would he come after you here? Why now?"

She shrugged. "He's been trying to kill me ever since. Maybe he thinks I can identify him."

"Wait. He's been trying to kill you all this time?"

"It seems so. He tried to break into my condo, but he set off my alarm. I always felt like someone was watching me. I knew I wouldn't be safe if I stayed in Cincinnati. I… had to get out of there."

"So that's why you came here?"

"After spending some time in a few other places, yes. But he found me at each location. I could sense when he was close."

"So this guy who murdered all those people didn't want any witnesses left behind." Andrew's words were more of a statement than a question.

Natalie nodded. "That's my guess."

"Did you get a good look at him?"

"Not really. He had a baseball hat on, and I didn't even try to make out his features. I just knew I needed to get away from him. Then outside last night, it was dark, and everything happened so fast." Her appetite began to wane as the conversation continued.

"So now you think this guy took your sister?"

A frown tugged at her lips. "I'm not sure."

"Why would he do that even?"

"Again, I'm not sure." Natalie had wrestled with those questions all morning.

Thankfully, just then their food was delivered.

Natalie needed a break from this conversation, and the breakfast in front of her would be the perfect distraction—even if she couldn't manage to eat it.

Except…as she glanced across the restaurant, she thought she saw a familiar face.

"Natalie?" Andrew asked as he followed her gaze.

"That man… I think I worked with him in Cincinnati."

* * *

As Andrew studied the man, the guy turned and looked at them.

Recognition lit his face, and he rose.

In several strides, he reached them. "Natalie! I didn't expect to see you here. What are the odds? You're looking good." His voice sobered as he said the last sentence.

"I wasn't expecting to see you here either, Nathan," Natalie croaked out.

"I love this area. I come whenever I can. I didn't realize you'd moved here."

She tugged at her collar. "I'm just visiting."

"I've been wondering about you and how you were doing after…" He didn't finish his statement. Instead, he said, "I didn't believe anything that Gary said about you."

Andrew watched as Natalie's eyes lit with confusion. "Gary? What do you mean?"

"You know…when he was telling everyone at the office that you didn't deserve that promotion. It simply wasn't true. I always thought he was just jealous."

"I… I see." Natalie rubbed the side of her face as if she didn't know what to say.

"I'm sorry. I thought you knew about that. Anyway, I'll let you get back to eating." Nathan had just turned to leave when Natalie called him.

He paused.

"I'd like to keep it under wraps that I'm here right now. If you wouldn't mind…"

He nodded. "I'll keep it quiet. Of course."

When he was gone, Andrew turned to Natalie. "Small world?"

"You can say that again."

"Who's this Gary guy?"

She shrugged. "Just a coworker. I had no idea he was badmouthing me."

"The business world is cutthroat."

"You can say that again. That is one thing I haven't missed these past few months. I hope Nathan keeps his word and doesn't tell people I'm here."

"I hope that as well."

As Andrew took a bite of his hash browns, he thought about Natalie's story.

Compassion welled inside him. He couldn't imagine going through what she'd been through. Trauma like that was difficult to get over.

As a police officer, he'd experienced life-threatening situations that had taken a toll on him. But he'd never been attacked by a dog. He'd never been hunted.

But knowing what he did now made him understand Natalie's actions. Her skittish nature. Her reaction last night to the man outside. Her paranoia about her sister.

She had every reason to be on edge.

What Andrew still wasn't sure about was why this guy might have followed Natalie to Gatlinburg and then abducted her sister. That puzzle piece didn't fit.

Then again, maybe Lexi had just taken off somewhere, and there were somehow two separate events going on right here that weren't connected. However, her smashed cell phone made that seem more unlikely.

But Andrew had learned not to take anything for granted. He made his decisions based on evidence, and right now he didn't have anything conclusive to work with.

He would keep searching for answers.

"Thank you for listening to all of this." Natalie's stunning blue-green eyes fluttered up to meet his. "I don't talk about this very often."

"I can see why. I can only imagine how painful this experience has been for you." Andrew poured some maple syrup on his pancakes, the sweet scent rising around him and bringing him a moment of comfort. "So how long were you in the hospital?"

"A week. I tried to go home to heal afterward but..." Natalie swallowed hard. "That's when the man showed up at my place. Thankfully, my alarm scared him away. But not before he left me a message."

"What kind of message?"

"He left an hourglass on my doorstep. He'd turned it upside down, letting the sand fall slowly to the bottom as if warning me my time was running out."

"Did you tell the police everything?" He took another bite of his hash browns, his jaw aching as he chewed. He ignored his discomfort, but it was a reminder of everything that had happened last night.

"I did. But I knew I couldn't stay in my condo anymore. It didn't feel safe, and I didn't want this guy to know where I was. So I went to stay at a friend's rental house in Michigan, and I didn't tell anyone where I was. I stayed for five weeks until I came inside one day and noticed some things had been moved. I knew he'd been there. So I ran. I went to a couple other places for a few nights until I ended up here." She picked at her food, suddenly not seeming hungry.

"That must have been terrifying."

"It was. It's strange how one instant can change everything, you know? One day, I was on top of the world and climbing the ladder to success. The next I was fighting for my life—and I have the scars to prove it." She pointed to her jaw.

"That's how life works sometimes, isn't it?" He could understand all too well.

"You know a lot about me, and I could really take a breather from talking about myself." Natalie took a bite of her crisp bacon. "What about you? What are you doing out here?"

Talking about himself was one thing Andrew didn't

want to do. But after everything Natalie had shared, he couldn't remain tightlipped.

"I'm staying at my grandparents' old cabin for a while," he started, cutting another piece of his pancake. He lifted it, and gooey syrup dripped from his fork. "I used to come here as a kid, and I loved it. In fact, they used to bring me to this restaurant to eat. I remember carving my initials under one of the tables. It's probably still here somewhere."

"Eating here must bring back some fond memories. But you work for the Nashville Police Department, right? Is this an extended vacation or something?" Natalie stared at him, curious.

Andrew's stomach clenched. He shouldn't be surprised that she asked. But it wasn't something he wanted to talk about yet.

"It's a long story," he started. "I know you've opened up to me a lot, and I should probably tell you more. But please believe me when I say I'm on leave, but it doesn't have anything to do with my integrity. There was an incident at the station, and I'm taking some time away right now."

Andrew's throat tightened at the words. That was over-simplifying the situation. He'd left out the betrayal and heartbreak that went along with it. Every time he thought he'd dealt with those emotions, something would happen to make him realize he hadn't.

Natalie glanced up at him, and he saw the questions in her gaze.

But she didn't ask anything else.

Instead, she ate a little more and glanced across the parkway.

As she did, her breath caught.

Andrew followed her gaze, curious to see what made her have that reaction.

He didn't see anything straightaway. Just traffic and a few pedestrians.

"Natalie? What is it?" he asked.

She pointed across the street. "I just saw a man standing over there staring at us."

"Did you recognize him?"

Natalie shook her head, her arms suddenly beginning to tremble. "No, but he was watching us. I'm sure of it."

Andrew shoved his plate away and rose. "Stay here. Rambo, stay."

Then before Natalie could object, he took off across the street.

This could be their best chance to find answers, and Andrew didn't want to blow it.

And if this was the guy who'd shot at him this morning and intended on harming Natalie…then that was even more reason to catch him now.

EIGHT

Natalie glanced down nervously at Rambo.

The dog sat up now, his ears alert.

But he didn't move.

When Andrew told him to stay, the dog most definitely listened.

She knew that dogs could be very faithful and loyal companions. In fact, until the dog attack incident had happened, Natalie had liked dogs and had even thought about getting one for herself.

Then everything had changed that night.

Every time Natalie closed her eyes, if she let herself, she remembered what it felt like to have those teeth dig into her flesh. She remembered the terror she felt. Remembered the certainty that she was going to die.

The man had intentionally let his dog maul her. As if he'd taken pleasure in the act.

The thought disgusted her. What kind of vile person would do that?

Why hadn't he just shot her like he had the other people at the party? Sure, he'd shot at her. But had that only been a warning shot? Had he missed on purpose? It was almost as if he had wanted her to suffer.

Her muscles tightened as she mentally relived the attack. Her heart began to pound harder. Her lungs squeezed.

She had to get herself under control. This was no time for a panic attack.

Drawing in a deep breath, she glanced across the street again.

Andrew had disappeared, which only heightened her anxiety.

She wanted to stand, to peer around the curve in the road to see where he had gone.

But she didn't dare move. Terror and bad memories kept her in place.

Instead, she lifted a prayer that Andrew would be safe.

Prayer was something Natalie had forgotten about until recently. She'd grown up in the church, but as her education and then career had begun to dominate her life, church had faded from her schedule.

She'd promised herself she'd go back one day. But that hadn't happened.

Until after her attack.

Unfortunately, sometimes it took heartaches in life to drive people back to the things that were most important. It was no different for Natalie.

She swallowed hard and rubbed the scar on her jaw again as she waited for Andrew to return.

She prayed that he wasn't hurt.

She had no idea who that man had been. But she was certain he'd been watching them.

He *could* have been the man who'd killed those executives. The one taunting her. Invading her nightmares.

He could also have Lexi. Had this guy taken Lexi to torment Natalie?

Or this could be something else totally different?

Could there be two separate crimes going on here? But what were the odds?

Her pulse started to speed again at all the possibilities.

Would she find out the truth before it was too late?

Her phone buzzed, and she glanced down.

Who would be texting her right now? She'd given strict instructions at her work not to contact her for any reason.

But when she looked at her phone, it wasn't a coworker or an employee. She had a text message from an unknown number. Her eyes skimmed the words.

Once bitten, twice shy.

The blood drained from her face at the implications of the message.

Andrew darted across the street and raced toward the man.

But the guy had a head start on him and was surprisingly fast. The watcher wove in and out of others on the sidewalk, causing cries of alarm.

Andrew tried to pace himself. He couldn't hurt anyone in his rush to catch this guy.

But he didn't want the man to get away either.

He tried to soak in the details of the man. His medium build and height. His lithe movements.

But the guy wore all black—including the ball cap that was pulled down low over his face. Andrew couldn't make out his features.

He did, however, match the description that Jim had given them of the man lingering behind the restaurant last night.

The man angled across the road, causing several drivers to throw on their brakes and lay on their horns.

The man didn't even flinch. He simply kept running, determined to get away.

Andrew followed. Dodging between vehicles, he raised his hand to get them to allow him through.

But the whole process had slowed him down.

He reached the sidewalk and paused.

Where had that man gone?

Andrew finally spotted him in a nearby parking lot. But the guy had gained too much distance on him.

As Andrew watched, the man jumped on a motorcycle—more of a dirt bike—and took off down a side road.

Andrew paused to catch his breath.

There was no way he'd catch him now.

He bit back a few choice words.

He'd been close, but the guy had gotten away.

Andrew returned to the restaurant, anxious to see Natalie with his own eyes and make sure she was okay. He hoped this wasn't some ploy to lure him away so someone else could move in and execute another phase of a sick plan.

Thankfully, he spotted Natalie sitting at the same table where he'd left her, looking rather anxious as she fiddled with the napkin in her lap.

Her eyes lit up when she saw him.

Andrew lowered himself into the chair across from her and caught his breath.

"Are you okay?" He stared at her face, looking for any signs of truth or deceit.

Natalie nodded before saying, "I'm okay. I mean, physically at least. Emotionally, well…that's a different story. What happened?"

He scowled and shook his head. "He got away."

She frowned before handing him her phone. "There's something you need to see. This came in right after you left."

He read the message there and felt the anger simmering in his blood.

The guy Andrew had been chasing couldn't have sent this. The man wouldn't have had the opportunity because he'd been running the whole time.

So who had? Were there two people in play here? Were they working together?

Obviously, whoever sent this either was involved with the incident with the executives and the dog attack, or they knew what happened and wanted to taunt Natalie.

Seemed like a lot of trouble to go through to play a sick game.

Either way, Andrew didn't like the way this was going.

If things kept escalating, someone was going to get hurt.

Despite his vows to remain low-key, it was becoming harder and harder to remain objective.

But he'd figure out a way to solve this one way or another.

Andrew quickly dropped some cash on the table and stood.

"I can get this," Natalie started as she reached for her purse.

"It's my treat this time. I think we need to go talk to the police."

"But doesn't Lexi have to be missing forty-eight hours before they'll do anything, or is that just a misconception people have?"

Andrew raised his shoulder in a half shrug and took Rambo's leash. "Normally, it's true. But in this case, we have that text message. I think we need to talk to them and see what we can find out. Then we'll go talk to this Frank guy."

Natalie nodded and stood also. "That sounds like a good plan. Thank you for breakfast."

"My pleasure."

They left the restaurant and began to walk.

"The police station is just around this next block," Andrew told her.

It wasn't far, but he remained guarded on their walk, looking for any other signs of trouble.

Thankfully, they didn't run into the man dressed in black again.

When they stepped inside the station, Andrew kept Rambo at his side. He knew that the dog may not be welcome, but he wasn't about to tie the canine up outside either. He'd keep the dog with him until someone told him he couldn't.

But no one seemed to give Rambo a second glance. Maybe they recognized a police dog when they saw one.

"Can I help you?" a middle-aged officer with dark hair who was stationed behind the front desk asked, his tone almost making it sound as if he were bored.

"We have a missing person to report," Andrew said.

"Have a seat in those chairs. I'll send someone to speak with you."

About fifteen minutes later, a thirty-something man wearing a button-up shirt and khakis stepped out, introduced himself as Detective Will Caruso, and nodded to a room off the side of the lobby.

The meeting room had a rectangular table pushed up against the wall, and a two-way mirror, making it look as if it doubled as an interrogation room.

Maybe it did. Either way, it gave them the space they needed to talk. But something in Andrew's gut told him this officer might not take any of this seriously.

For now, he'd give him the benefit of the doubt.

They all sat around the table, and Caruso pulled a pad of paper from his back pocket. "What can I help you with?"

Andrew nodded to Natalie, indicating she should take the lead.

She sucked in a deep breath—no doubt drawing in her courage.

"It's my sister." Her voice cracked as she started. "She's missing, and I fear she's in danger."

"What's your sister's full name?"

"It's Lexi. Lexi Pearson."

The detective's gaze seemed to harden. "I wasn't aware Lexi had a sister."

"You know her?" Surprise stretched through her voice.

"I do. Are you sure she's missing? Because she's the type who will leave without saying a word."

Andrew's gut tightened.

He didn't like where this conversation was going, and he feared his initial impression of this guy had been spot-on.

Natalie stared at Detective Caruso as he sat in front of her, his words echoing in her mind.

"What is *that* supposed to mean?" she finally asked.

The detective narrowed his eyes as if her question annoyed him. "Lexi has disappeared before. More than once, in fact."

Her back stiffened. "When?"

"A few weeks ago, she didn't show up for work for a couple of days. Her manager called in a report. We sent our patrol officers out to look for her. We found her passed out near the bus station. Another time, she called the police herself. She was at a rental cabin. She'd woken up there alone and didn't know where she was. Apparently, she'd gone home with someone. He'd left that morning to go on a hike and let her sleep in, and she couldn't remember most of it."

"But her car was left in the parking lot where she works," Natalie started. "She wouldn't—"

Caruso cut her off with a shake of his head. "That doesn't mean anything. People get rides with other people all the time. It doesn't mean that any type of crime happened."

There had to be more to this. "But—"

"Your sister likes to live life on the edge," he interrupted again, that annoyed sharpness to his voice. "My guess is that Lexi met someone at the restaurant last night and decided to go her own way. She's not used to having someone around to hold her down or have to report to."

Natalie bristled at the words *hold her down*. That was what Lexi used to always tell her—that Natalie wanted to hold her back, to be a cosmic killjoy. She'd say Natalie was trying to act like her mother.

Natalie had only been trying to look out for her sister.

But that had driven a wedge between them.

Caruso tilted his head to the side. "Am I right? I mean, you haven't been here that long, have you? I'm sure I would've seen you around town."

"I came here less than two weeks ago."

"Well, Lexi isn't used to answering to anybody."

"You sound like you know this from experience." Maybe Natalie shouldn't have spoken the words, but she didn't like this guy telling her what her sister was like, nor did she like the fact that he was dismissing her.

"Tell me I'm wrong," Detective Caruso challenged.

Natalie wanted to argue with him, but she couldn't. The detective was telling the truth.

That sounded *exactly* like her sister.

But in Natalie's gut, she knew there was more to the story.

She thought about that text she'd received. She remembered the tattered seats in Lexi's car and her smashed phone.

Should she mention those things?

Before she could think about it, Andrew spoke up. "Natalie also received a text message."

Caruso's eyebrows shot up. "From Lexi?"

"We don't know who sent it," Andrew explained. "But it is significant."

Natalie pulled out her phone and brought up the message.

But the detective shrugged. "I'm not sure how that indicates someone took your sister."

Natalie swallowed. "Once bitten? Twice shy? I was attacked by a dog not long ago. This is clearly a threat."

"Maybe. Maybe not. But it doesn't sound like it has anything to do with Lexi."

Natalie let out a frustrated breath, but before she could explain her reasoning, Andrew slipped something out of his pocket.

"We also found this underneath Lexi's vehicle." Andrew slid Lexi's broken phone across the table.

"And this is?" Detective Caruso didn't touch it.

"Lexi's cell phone," Natalie answered. "She would never leave it behind. Something happened to her."

Caruso rubbed a hand down his face and cleared his throat. "Look, she's probably lost two other cell phones since I've known her. She's not the most responsible person."

"So you're just going to discount everything we're saying here?" Natalie felt anger rising within her. "Something has happened to my sister. Don't let whatever personal problem you seem to have with her get in the way of your job."

Caruso suddenly grew very still, and his eyes narrowed.

But before Caruso could speak, Andrew slipped the phone back into his pocket. "Natalie, I think we're about done here."

"But…" Natalie looked at Andrew as she started to argue with him. But something in his gaze stopped her.

Maybe he was right. Caruso didn't seem to be open to anything they were saying.

If Natalie pressed the issue, there would be a lot more questions about her past. In fact, Caruso could even draw attention to what had happened to her. The last thing Natalie wanted was any reporters finding her here.

Then again, Natalie had come here so the killer wouldn't find her.

But it seemed more and more obvious that he already had.

An ache began pulsing in her head at the thought.

Andrew squeezed her shoulder, jolting her from her thoughts.

She looked over at him and slowly released her breath.

Even though Andrew didn't know her, he seemed to sense her distress. He had a natural inclination to bring comfort to others. She'd been able to see that in his mannerisms, in the way he treated his dog even.

Maybe he was a godsend in this whole situation.

She looked back up at the detective. He tapped his fingers against the desk as if he had better things to do.

There was no way she could trust this guy to help her. He seemed to already have his mind made up when it came to Lexi.

She'd be better off investigating herself and relying on Andrew—provided he still wanted to help.

No, Natalie wasn't going to count on the police to step up.

Caruso stood, clearly ready to finish this meeting. "Come back in forty-eight hours if you still haven't heard from her. Then we'll file a missing persons case."

A lot could happen in forty-eight hours, Natalie mused.

Lexi could come back by then.

Or she could be dead by then.

Natalie couldn't let that happen.

She looked to Andrew for encouragement. But she only found a reflection of her own thoughts. He didn't look any more encouraged than she felt.

Disappointment and anxiety mingled in her chest until she felt as if she might throw up.

NINE

Andrew didn't like the way that conversation had gone down.

Didn't like the way the detective had dismissed Natalie's concerns.

He supposed another part of him understood. Based on what Andrew knew about Lexi's personality, this event may not be all that unusual.

But the detective had been condescending, and that was what bothered him the most.

Andrew had been tempted to show the detective his own badge. To show Caruso he was on an even playing field. But he hadn't wanted to overstep. It had been Natalie's opportunity to speak to the detective.

Still, if Andrew had a chance, he might talk to the detective one-on-one later—not in front of Natalie. Right now, she already seemed on the verge of falling apart.

As soon as they stepped outside, Andrew gently touched Natalie's back to lead her toward his truck. "It's after ten o'clock. Let's go talk to Frank."

She nodded. "Should we call him first?"

"Probably a good idea." Andrew paused near the station doorway, pulled out his phone and dialed the man's number. But there was no answer.

"What now?" Natalie asked.

Andrew typed something into his phone. "I'd still like to check things out. If he's not answering, then maybe we should pay him a visit at home and see if we can wake him up."

A few minutes later, Andrew had the man's address. Perfect.

They continued toward Andrew's Bronco. But Natalie's steps faltered when she glanced at the vehicle.

"What is that?" Andrew muttered as he stared at something on his hood.

"It's an hourglass," she muttered. "Just like the one left for me at my house in Cincinnati."

Andrew's thoughts began to spin, and he glanced around.

That man…he'd been here. He wanted to taunt them.

Andrew liked this situation less and less all the time.

But right now, he needed to find some answers.

"We should tell the detective," he started.

Natalie shook her head. "No. I don't want to explain everything to him all over again. Not yet."

"It's your choice." He understood her reasoning—but she couldn't keep things to herself at the expense of her safety either.

He'd give her more time to make up her mind before he tried to convince her.

A few minutes later, after collecting the hourglass and putting it into a bag, Andrew and Natalie had woven through the city streets and turned off the main highway.

The side road they took climbed up the Smoky Mountains and wound around several tight curves until they pulled up to a brick ranch house. The place seemed out of place in the rustic environment.

Most of the houses in this area were either cabins or mountain chalets, but Frank's looked as if it had been ripped from suburban America and placed on a level lot on the side of the mountain.

The brick was red with a pinkish tint. The front of the house was flat with only two windows. It had three steps, and a flimsy metal railing leading to the front door. The garage door had been painted beige, but one of the panels was hanging sideways.

Andrew instructed Rambo to stay in the car. It was a nice day outside so the canine would be fine. But he did crack the window to give the dog some fresh air.

Then he and Natalie walked to the front door. An expensive-looking black Lexus sat in the driveway so Andrew could only assume someone was home.

He knocked on the door, and a moment later a tired-looking man with tousled, curly red hair answered.

"Can I help you?" He glanced at both of them before his gaze stopped on Natalie. He observed her a moment as if trying to place her.

She and Lexi *did* look similar once you got past their hair and the way they dressed.

Andrew would be able to tell them apart in a heartbeat. Natalie's entire countenance was different than her sister's. But he understood why others might do a double take.

"I'm Natalie Pearson, Lexi's sister," she started. "She didn't come home last night. I'm looking for her, and I was hoping to ask you a few questions."

He glanced around as if looking for anyone else lingering nearby. Then he stepped outside and closed the door. He wore a short sleeve shirt but he didn't seem to be bothered by the winter chill in the air.

Frank crossed his muscular arms and waited, occasionally glancing at Andrew.

Andrew introduced himself and then tried to get a read on the guy. He seemed fairly laid-back.

"What do you need to know?" Frank asked, appearing casual and friendly.

But was there a touch of nerves to his tone?

"Did you see Lexi last night?" Natalie started.

"I did. Nothing unusual about her shift. It was a normal night at the restaurant, and I believe she left about one thirty."

"Did any other employees leave at the same time?" Andrew asked.

Frank thought about the question a moment before shaking his head. "I don't think so. There weren't very many of us still working at that hour. But she was the first to leave, and the rest of us stayed behind and finished clearing the tables and washing the dishes."

"There weren't any men around her giving her special attention or waiting for her until she left?"

Andrew knew Natalie needed some answers—she needed *something* to grasp on to.

The question was, would this guy help her find those answers?

Frank shrugged. "Not that I can remember. It was a busy night, and I didn't have a lot of time to pay attention to stuff like that. But there was no one over the top. I would've definitely noticed that."

Disappointment entered her gaze. She glanced at Andrew as if silently asking for help.

"Her car is still in the parking lot," Andrew interjected. "Has Lexi ever left it behind before?"

Frank nodded, an almost apologetic look in his eyes. "Yeah, she has. A few times. I always tell Lexi to be careful. But she's a big girl. She can make her own decisions. And there's nothing I can do to stop her."

Andrew frowned.

Based on what everybody had told them, it wasn't looking good as far as building a case to find Lexi.

Maybe he shouldn't have, but he reached out and squeezed Natalie's shoulder. He wished he could do more to help her find answers, but for now it seemed their options were limited.

As Natalie walked away from Frank's house and back toward the truck, she tried to find some semblance of hope. Time was ticking away, and she knew what that meant.

The longer Lexi was missing, the less likely it was she'd be found alive.

She'd seen enough true crime shows to know that was the case.

Without the police's help, she had to investigate on her own. But answers were too slow coming in. What if she was moving in the wrong direction and wasting valuable time?

Andrew would tell her if that was the case, right? He was experienced. She could trust his guidance.

So why did she still feel so anxious?

"There is one thing," Frank called.

She and Andrew both stopped and turned toward him, waiting for whatever he had remembered.

"You might want to talk to that guy she's been out with a few times lately."

Natalie cleared her throat. "Who is that?"

"Some guy who works at the police station. Detective Caruso, I think."

Natalie sucked in a breath.

Wait…the detective Natalie and Andrew had talked to at the station had dated Lexi?

Why hadn't he given any indications of that when they were talking to him?

That didn't sound right. Lexi hadn't mentioned it to Natalie, and she normally stayed far away from anyone affiliated with law enforcement. She'd had too many run-ins with them in the past.

Tension bubbled inside her.

She and Andrew exchanged a look.

"Do you know what happened between them?" Natalie asked. "Are they still dating?"

"Not anymore." Frank shrugged. "She dumped him. He wasn't very happy about it. But Lexi didn't care. You know how she is."

Yes, Natalie did. Lexi could break up with a guy and not think anything of it.

"One more thing." Frank adjusted his arms, which were still crossed over his chest. "We do have some security cameras behind the restaurant. They're pretty well hidden—in fact, they look like birdhouses."

Hope swelled inside her. Maybe there was something on that video feed!

"Anyway, I'm the only one allowed to access them because we've had problems with some employees messing around with them in the past," Frank continued. "But I can meet you there around three and review the footage with you. I just gotta do a couple of things around here first."

"That sounds great," Natalie rushed. "Thank you."

Natalie and Andrew climbed into Andrew's truck, and he backed out of the driveway.

Natalie's thoughts still raced as she reviewed their conversation.

"Maybe the security camera footage will show us something," Andrew said.

"We can only hope. Right now, it's the only thing that we have to go on—unless we want to confront Detective Caruso about his relationship with Lexi."

Andrew frowned. "I'm not sure that would be a good idea. I don't like the fact he wasn't forthcoming with this information."

"I don't like it either. So, what do we do now? We still have two and a half hours to kill until Frank can meet us."

"That's not really enough time to go back home and do anything. We might as well hang around Gatlinburg and see if there's anyone else we can talk to about Lexi."

Natalie didn't miss how Andrew glanced in his rearview mirror several times.

She craned her neck to see the road behind them. "What's going on?"

A dark SUV with tinted windows followed behind them. The driver was following close—maybe too close.

"I don't like the way this guy is driving." Andrew's jaw hardened. "Some people don't know how to drive in the mountains. But I'm wondering if there's more to this than that."

"You mean…you think he's…" Natalie couldn't even finish the statement.

"I'm not going to assume anything. But we need to be careful." His gaze slid to the rearview mirror again as tension visibly rippled through his muscles.

Natalie leaned back in her seat and gripped the armrest beside her. "In the police academy…did you have offensive driving lessons? Or whatever it's called."

"Every two years I take an emergency vehicle operation course. It covers all the standards. High-speed pursuit. Safety. Emergency driving techniques. That kind of thing." He glanced her way. "I've got this, Natalie. It's going to be okay."

She wanted to believe he could handle any circumstance they might find themselves in. He sounded confident enough.

But what if it was the killer? Would he be as bold as to follow them on this narrow mountain road?

It didn't seem to fit his MO. With the past crimes, he'd

shot the executives and had his dog attack her. Would he also resort to running them off the road?

She could only guess. Natalie really knew very little about the man. Only that he was dangerous and sadistic.

Anyone who would sic his dog on someone and leave them for dead was twisted.

At once, images of all the executives lying dead with gunshot wounds in that living room filled her mind. She squeezed her eyes closed, trying to shut out the memories of their lifeless bodies. Of the scent of blood. At the horror that had occurred there.

It felt useless.

It was a scene she'd never, ever forget. Natalie had tried to scrub the images from her mind more times than she could count.

But it never worked.

Just as the memories tried to pummel her again, she jerked forward.

She sucked in a breath.

That SUV had hit them, hadn't it? On purpose.

Andrew gripped the steering wheel as he fought to maintain control of his truck.

As he did, Natalie lifted up a prayer for protection.

Andrew didn't like where this was going.

The driver behind them was definitely targeting them. That nudge hadn't been accidental or even careless driving.

He pressed the accelerator, but he knew it wasn't safe to go fast on this road. It was narrow, with the mountain climbing on one side and dropping off on the other. And it was curvy, making it nearly impossible to see what was coming just ahead.

Accelerating right now might help them to escape one danger, but it would only create another.

The SUV nudged them again.

Andrew muttered under his breath. There was nowhere to go here. It was either stay on the paved road, crash into the mountain, or fall from the drop-off on the other side.

He only liked the first option. But the odds weren't looking good.

The vehicle's engine quieted behind him.

He glanced in the rearview mirror again and saw that the other driver had backed off.

What…?

But the next instant, the SUV's driver gunned the engine and charged toward them again.

Andrew braced himself for whatever was about to happen and prayed he'd learned from the police training and was skilled enough to handle the situation.

The other driver jetted into the lane beside him.

Andrew prayed that there were no other cars coming. If there were, there would be a head-on collision.

Then he felt another ram.

His truck screeched along the rock wall beside them.

He pumped the brakes as he tried to regain control of the vehicle.

As they jerked to a stop, the SUV beside him squealed away.

His heart pounding, Andrew squinted as he tried to get a license plate.

But it was no use.

Because there was no license plate on the SUV.

TEN

Natalie felt her head spinning as she tried to comprehend what had just happened.

Andrew touched her shoulder. "Are you okay?"

She blinked several times, trying to gather herself. "I think so. You?"

He nodded.

Then he glanced in the back at Rambo.

The dog was panting—clearly nervous—but he was okay.

He let out a little whine before lying down in the seat.

"That was close." Andrew ran a hand through his hair. "Too close."

"That person wanted to send a message."

"You can say that again. Did you get a glimpse of him?"

Natalie shook her head. "I tried, but everything happened so fast, and his windows were tinted."

She glanced at the front of Andrew's truck. There were several dents and crinkles in it, but the situation could have been much, much worse.

However, she wasn't sure if she'd be able to get her door open.

The rock wall had scraped her side of the vehicle.

"Let me check this out before we do anything else." Andrew turned on his emergency blinkers, popped the hood and climbed out. He walked toward the front of the vehicle and checked out the engine. He did something on the other side, while Natalie stayed where she was. She would have to climb over the console to get out his door in order to exit right now.

In fact, as she looked over, she could see the moisture on the rock wall. Saw some moss growing there. Smelled the wet rock.

That's how close she was. Only a few inches difference and…

She didn't want to think about it.

She shivered.

That had been too close.

A moment later, Andrew climbed back into the truck.

"Everything looks okay with the engine. I think it's mostly just body damage. Let me see if I can start this bad boy back up and see if we can get into town."

Natalie held her breath as he tried the ignition.

The first time, nothing happened.

But on the second try, the engine roared to life.

Relief filled her.

She prayed Andrew was correct, that it was just body damage. She'd already nearly gotten him killed again. She was on the verge of upending his life. Now she'd ruined his truck—his pride and joy, right behind Rambo.

A moment later, Andrew eased back onto the road.

The truck still was operational!

Thank You, Jesus!

But next time, she realized she and Andrew might not be so blessed.

Andrew hadn't meant to get himself involved in something like this.

But now it was too late. He was in too deep.

And he wouldn't be able to rest until he knew what was going on right now.

Someone desperately wanted to silence Natalie—for good.

He wasn't sure how Lexi tied in with all of what was happening.

But she did somehow. It could very well simply be that someone had taken Lexi to threaten Natalie.

But he and Natalie still needed more answers. Yes, he and Natalie. Somehow, they felt like a team.

Since he wasn't working with her in a strictly professional manner, he didn't need to keep up the walls he usually did on the job. As a result, he allowed himself to feel the bond that was naturally forming between the two of them.

It almost felt like even if this crime hadn't drawn them together, they would have still somehow found each other and clicked.

He hadn't felt like this many times in his life—and definitely not since Sarah. Things had ended between them nearly eight months ago. His name had been raked through the mud so deep he'd been suspended.

Then he'd come here to the Tennessee mountains to recover.

Something about the mountains always soothed him. Coming here to regroup had been the right choice.

"Should we tell the police about what just happened?" Natalie asked.

He sighed. "I should call it in. I just don't have much confidence in Caruso."

"That makes two of us."

He and Natalie pulled back up at the Alpine Bistro and Barbecue. The parking lot was halfway full now as the lunch crowd started to trickle in.

Once his truck was parked, he called the local police

and reported what had happened. They took note of the incident and said they'd look for a vehicle matching the description of the one that had run them off the road.

When he ended the call, Andrew leaned back in his seat a moment.

He wanted to have more confidence in the police department than he actually had. Caruso was the number one reason. But the bad feeling he had about Caruso shouldn't automatically extend to everyone on the force here.

Andrew, of all people, understood how important it was to give people a chance to prove themselves.

"What are we doing now?" Natalie stared at the building with a frown.

"I thought we could see if Rambo could pick up on your sister's scent. That would give us something to do while we wait until Frank gets here."

She glanced back at the dog. "That would be amazing."

Andrew noted the tone of Natalie's voice had changed a bit. She didn't sound as scared of Rambo as she'd first been.

"Dogs are amazing," he told her. "Humans only have about five million scent sensors. Dogs have closer to a hundred million."

Her eyes widened. "That *is* amazing."

"It really is." Andrew rubbed Rambo's head. "The world's a better place with dogs like Rambo in it."

"Well, maybe you're not such a bad guy after all." Natalie tentatively rubbed the dog's head.

Seeing Natalie warm up to Rambo brought Andrew a surprising sense of satisfaction. Rambo was a great dog—loyal, protective, smart.

Andrew had always thought that everyone should have a dog—a nonjudgmental companion who was always there and would listen without interruption. It was a shame when one bad apple ruined the rest, as the saying went.

"I figure this is worth a shot," Andrew said. "But Rambo will need something that smells like her."

"I'm sure Lexi has something in her car. But I don't have the key."

Andrew reached into his glove box and pulled out a long, narrow metal stick. "I can fix that. It's a long reach tool. I used them on occasion back in Nashville."

Natalie's eyes widened as if she was impressed.

He slid out from the front seat and then extended his hand to help her.

Carefully, Natalie climbed over the console and out his door. Once she was steady on her feet, Andrew retrieved Rambo from the back.

Natalie paced over to her side of the truck and cringed when she saw the scrapes on the blue paint. "That isn't going to be a cheap fix."

"Insurance should cover most of it." The last thing Andrew wanted was for Natalie to feel responsible for the damage to his truck. He knew she already felt guilty over the incident in the woods last night. He'd caught her staring at his swollen jaw.

They went over to Lexi's car.

Andrew jimmied the lock and opened the door.

"Careful what you touch," he told her. "Just in case."

Natalie nodded and opened the glove box in her sister's car. "Lexi won't go anywhere without her hairbrush." She held it up. "Will this work?"

"It's perfect." Andrew took it from her and then held it to Rambo's nose. After a moment, he commanded, "Search."

A second later, Rambo began pulling Andrew to the woods behind the restaurant.

Andrew felt a thrill of excitement rush through him.

There was something he loved about being on the job.

Being a cop was something he'd always wanted to

do and making detective had made him feel as if all his dreams had come true.

Then when he'd been introduced to Rambo and the two of them had learned to work as a team, everything had felt complete.

Right now, the canine led him toward the woods behind the restaurant.

Andrew wasn't sure how far they would be able to go on foot back here. The terrain was rocky, and it eventually led down to a creek. On the other side of the creek, the mountains rose steeply before reaching an area with rental homes perched high above them.

"Are you going to be okay keeping up?" he asked Natalie.

"I'll be fine," she said. "I want to see where Rambo leads us."

But her voice trembled as she said the words.

Anyone in her situation would feel a little nervous right now. Nervous about the journey. About what they might find at the end of it. Or that they wouldn't find anything.

They reached an especially rocky area that led toward the creek, and he paused, offering her his hand. Natalie slipped her hand in his, and he helped her down the area.

He couldn't help but notice how soft and slim her fingers were.

Just like he couldn't help noticing the faint scent of flowers that wafted from her when the wind blew. Daisies, if he had to guess.

It was a nice scent. One he wouldn't mind indulging in.

But that wouldn't be appropriate.

Not only did he hardly know Natalie, but he wasn't looking to date. It appeared she wasn't either. The two of them were simply together now because of current circumstances. He'd be wise to remember that.

But Andrew would also be lying if he said that there wasn't something about the woman that fascinated him.

He continued down toward the water. As he did, he scanned everything around him.

There was a good chance that the person who'd run them off the road could have followed them here. This driver could have waited in a nearby lot until Andrew and Natalie emerged from the backroads and then kept a safe distance behind them.

Andrew hadn't seen anything. He'd been keeping his eyes open.

But still, he didn't want to assume the person behind this was careless. In fact, it seemed to be quite the opposite. For that reason, Andrew needed to be on guard.

Rambo pulled him until they reached the water. He continued sniffing along the creek, hot on the trail.

Water would make this more complicated. Though dogs could still track through a river or stream, it wasn't as easy.

Rambo stopped near a rock wall.

He sniffed but didn't move.

"What's going on?" Natalie paused beside him, sucking in deep breaths from the fast walk.

Andrew almost didn't want to admit what was happening. But he couldn't keep the truth from her.

"I think Lexi must have climbed up there." Andrew nodded.

"So Rambo lost the scent?" Disappointment sounded in her voice.

"Not necessarily. I'll see if I can find a way to the top. Stay here."

He and Rambo climbed around the rocky outcropping, reached the top, and walked several more feet.

But the scent ended in a gravel parking lot.

Andrew bit back a frown and made his way back to Natalie.

He explained the situation to her.

Her shoulders slumped. "Are you sure? Isn't there anything we can do?"

He frowned. "I'm sorry, Natalie. We could try and follow the tire tracks leading away from the parking lot, but they could go on for miles."

ELEVEN

Natalie paused by the creek and looked around.

She tried to imagine Lexi here.

But it would have been late at night and pitch-black out here when she disappeared.

"Why would someone have brought Lexi out here just to lead her to another parking lot and go somewhere else? It just doesn't make sense," she murmured. "She wouldn't have walked out here alone, that's for sure. Not of her own free will."

Andrew glanced around. "It is strange, isn't it? Your sister didn't strike me as the outdoorsy type. In fact, when I met her, I was surprised she'd gotten a cabin out here where it was so secluded."

"I always thought it was strange too." Natalie picked up a smooth river stone and rubbed it between her fingers. "She's more of the type to get an apartment so she could be around a lot of other people and hang out. She isn't exactly the solitary type. That was always more me."

"Does she like to hike at all?"

"No. Definitely not." Natalie glanced around again. "Which is why I know in my heart that if Rambo was right at all, and Lexi was out here…it's because someone forced her to be out here. Are you sure that Rambo knows what he's doing? No offense but…"

Andrew nodded. "If Rambo led us this way, it was for a reason. Lexi was down here."

"Then that settles it. Lexi was abducted."

Andrew's eyebrows shot up. "That's a strong statement."

Natalie sucked in another gulp of air as she tried to catch her breath.

"Why don't we sit down for a moment?" Andrew nodded to a large rock beside the creek. "It'll do us both good just to take a moment to catch our breaths."

She nodded and lowered herself onto the cold stone.

Beside her, the rippling waters brought her a measure of comfort.

A memory of her family coming to a stream like this on vacation hit her. They'd had lunch and skipped rocks across the water—until a black bear had emerged on the other side of the stream and sent them scrambling back to their car.

Back then, she and Lexi had been tight. Best friends.

She wished that hadn't changed.

Natalie found herself searching the stream, looking for any signs Lexi had passed through here. Rambo was starting to get restless, but she wasn't ready to leave the area yet. Part of her hoped if she stayed here just a while longer that maybe she'd be able to figure out what happened to her sister or find a clue.

As the sunlight peeked through the branches above, something gleamed below her. She reached between the rocks and picked up the object.

A hoop earring—just like the ones Lexi loved to wear. Her stomach dropped. "Oh no."

Part of her had still been holding out hope Rambo had been wrong.

Not anymore.

"Is that your sister's?" Andrew asked.

"I can't say for sure, but it looks like hers."

They exchanged a glance.

Losing an earring indicated to Natalie that a struggle had gone down. If Lexi had simply dropped it, she would have noticed her earring coming off.

A bad feeling continued to brew in Natalie's gut.

"Don't lose hope." Andrew's voice sounded low and reassuring.

She nodded, even though she wasn't sure not losing hope was possible.

She desperately wanted to reverse time back to when things were going well. Before walking in on the killings. Before Lexi had disappeared. Back to when her career was going well, and she had a nice life in Cincinnati.

But she couldn't. Lexi being missing kept her in place—and maybe that was exactly what someone had planned.

Rambo suddenly growled just before a loud bark came from the woods.

The next moment, a German shepherd mix bounded through the trees, charging straight toward Natalie.

Andrew saw the dog running their way.

He heard the terror in Natalie's voice as she screamed.

He rose to his feet and placed himself between Natalie and the oncoming dog.

Where had the canine come from?

It didn't matter right now. He just needed to make sure that everyone was safe.

He held out his hand, palm flat as he tried to block the dog.

Rambo sat beside him, a low growl coming from him as he seemed to anticipate that the dog might be aggressive.

"Whoa." Andrew kept his voice deep and low. "It's okay, boy."

Andrew remained tense as he waited to see what the animal would do next.

The dog crept closer, clearly curious.

Then he stopped. Sniffed. Looked around.

Finally, the canine sat in front of Andrew and looked up at him obediently.

"Good boy," Andrew murmured, trying to keep the dog calm.

A moment later, a young man and a woman came crashing through the woods after him. "Fido!"

The couple stopped near the dog, obviously out of breath. The woman held a leash and collar in her hands.

The dog must have slipped away from them.

"I'm so sorry." The woman's words came out fast. "Fido has never done that before. I thought his collar was tight enough…"

She slipped it back on him and then gave the dog a scolding.

As the woman glanced at Natalie, she must have noticed how terrified she looked.

"He's nice," the woman insisted. "He's never bitten anybody. He's just a little overly friendly sometimes. I'm sorry."

As Andrew glanced at Natalie, he saw the trembling claiming her body.

She was clearly reliving her attack.

Her reaction was totally normal for anyone who'd been through what she had.

"We didn't mean to interrupt you," the man said. "It won't happen again. I promise."

Andrew shifted, his thoughts racing. "Before you go, if you don't mind me asking, do you come here often?"

"We've been here a few times," the man said as he nodded. "Are you lost?"

"No, we're good. I was just wondering…have you seen anything unusual lately in this area?"

The man and woman glanced at each other and seemed to think about it before shaking their heads.

"I can't say we have," the man said. "What kind of unusual thing are you referring to? Some kind of animal been causing trouble?"

"No, nothing like that."

"Then what is it?" The woman spoke up as she placed her hand over her heart. "I watched this true crime show last night. It was about criminals that escaped from prison. They hid in a national park, killing any hikers they came across and stealing their supplies as they made their way up to Canada. Is that what's happening? Is it safe to be out here?"

The man with her looked at her. "We're nowhere near Canada. You do know that, right?"

She squinted at him. "Of course I do. I was talking about the escaped prisoners, not Canada specifically."

Before they could get into a heated debate, Andrew interrupted. "It's no more dangerous out here than usual, I suppose. I haven't heard of any prison breaks lately."

"Lately?" The woman gasped and looked at her hiking partner. "I told you we shouldn't come out here without bear spray."

"Here we go again." The man sighed.

"Thanks for your time," Andrew said, noting Natalie's stiff posture. She was still terrified from when the dog ran up to her, wasn't she?

The couple glanced at each other again and then they took their dog and walked back through the woods.

Andrew waited until they were out of sight before sitting down beside Natalie on the rock again.

"Well, that didn't go over so well, did it?" he said, hoping to lighten the mood.

When it didn't work, he slipped an arm around her, sensing she needed something to ground her right now.

He knew she might reject his comfort, but that was okay. He had to at least try.

"It's okay," Andrew murmured. "You're okay now."

To his surprise, Natalie leaned into him.

Her entire body quivered.

"The dog's not going to hurt you," he said. "He's gone."

But Natalie still didn't say anything.

Had she gone into a state of shock?

It was a real possibility.

"I need you to breathe," he murmured. "Take a deep breath. Can you do that for me?"

She didn't respond, so he repeated his instructions.

Finally, Natalie seemed to jolt back to the present. She sucked in several quick breaths.

"Breathe in and hold it. Count to five. Then release. It's going to be okay."

She did as Andrew had asked. Finally, a few moments of guided breathing later, she looked at him. Her face was still pale, and her limbs were trembling, but she looked better.

Without thinking, Andrew pulled her closer until she nestled her head between his neck and shoulder.

Then he held her until she was ready to move.

Natalie tried to get her racing heart under control as she and Andrew—and Rambo—made their way back to the parking lot.

Her thoughts still reeled after seeing that German shepherd mix racing toward her.

Would she ever get over this fear?

She wasn't sure.

Whenever she saw a dog, her entire body tensed as she anticipated pain.

Well, every dog but Rambo. That canine was starting to grow on her.

Still, right now, all she wanted was to sit down and compose herself.

"How about if we grab a light lunch while we're waiting for Frank to get here?" Andrew asked after they got back to the restaurant's parking lot. "I know we ate breakfast not long ago, but since we're here anyway, we could go inside Alpine and take a look around. Plus, eating here would give us an opportunity to ask questions."

"That's a good idea."

Natalie wasn't hungry and wasn't sure if she could even eat. But she did want to get inside the restaurant and check out the place for herself. They might as well make good use of their time.

A few minutes later, they were seated in an outdoor area with heaters, just like at the other restaurant. It was the only place Rambo was allowed. But the waitress had even gotten the dog some water, which Rambo happily lapped beside them.

As Natalie glanced at the menu, her ear caught something in the distance. She looked up at a TV perched in the corner under an awning and watched the commercial there.

"Have you been thinking about checking out some new mouthwash?" Andrew asked.

She let out a chuckle, finally beginning to relax. "Why? Do I need it?"

His face heated. "I… No. It's the commercial. You were watching it."

Natalie enjoyed making him squirm a little. "I'm teasing. I know what you meant."

This time Andrew let out a little laugh.

He'd surprised her today. His concern and compassion had been touching. He didn't flinch when he saw her scar. He didn't look at her like she was crazy or like he wanted to run for his life.

Unlike Philip...her boyfriend who'd fled at the first sign of hard times.

He'd loved living the good life with her. But that was as deep as he'd gone.

Surface-level relationships wouldn't cut it in the long run.

Natalie had been totally wrong about him. Or maybe she'd never truly opened her eyes. Maybe she hadn't wanted to see the truth about her handsome boyfriend.

She'd ignored the red flags.

That had been a mistake.

She swallowed hard and met Andrew's gaze. "I was actually in charge of that commercial. The one about the mouthwash."

Andrew raised his eyebrows. "Impressive."

"It's one of my favorites. I really do love advertising." Just thinking about it lifted her spirits and helped ground her.

"It's good to love what you do. I really love my job too."

Natalie had more questions for Andrew about his time in Nashville, but she didn't ask. She sensed he didn't want to talk about it, and she figured whatever had happened wasn't any of her business.

"Tell me about the ad campaign you were working on with those execs who were murdered," Andrew said.

She shifted, not expecting the question. "It was for a diabetes drug. We did an advertising campaign where we interviewed people whose lives had been changed by the medication. I really enjoyed working on the project."

"No friction with anyone on the team?"

Natalie thought about it a minute before shaking her head. "No, not that I can think of. Although, I suppose Gary really had wanted to win that account."

"That's probably why he was badmouthing you at the

office." Andrew leaned on the table. "Did you ever exchange words with him?"

"Not directly. I kept my opinions to myself. I didn't like his methods. He tried to undermine me, but thankfully everyone seemed to see through his tactics."

"Was he the type to hold grudges?"

"Honestly, I never really paid that much attention to him. I'm not entirely sure what the man is capable of."

Andrew nodded. "You got along with the execs?"

She nodded. "They were all great. It was easy to work with them. There was mutual respect between us. I listened to their ideas, and they listened to mine."

Before they could talk more, the waitress appeared again, ready to take their orders. The woman was Lexi's age, tattooed, and had an uninhibited air about her.

After noting her peanut allergy to the waitress, Natalie ordered some soup for herself, and Andrew ordered a club sandwich and fries.

Before the waitress—her name was Mandy—walked away, Natalie asked, "Say, do you know my sister by chance?"

Mandy turned and studied Natalie a minute. "Who's your sister?"

"Lexi Pearson."

"I thought you looked familiar." She nodded slowly as realization rolled over her. "Yes, of course, I know Lexi. She should be coming in a few hours for her shift."

"Have you talked to her today?"

Mandy shook her head. "No. Why?"

"Did you work with her at all yesterday?"

Mandy shifted and moved her tray to the other side. "As a matter of fact, yes. Our shift overlapped by a couple of hours. Is something going on?"

"She didn't come home last night, and I'm getting concerned about her. Did you see anything strange going on in the restaurant during your shift?" Natalie continued.

Mandy's expression tensed as if the question had caught her off guard.

"Anything strange?" She stared off in the distance, as if thinking. "There was one man here last night who seemed a little off."

Natalie's breath caught. "What do you mean?"

"I mean, he came in by himself, and he sat in the corner, just kind of watching everybody for a couple of hours. I mean, it's fine if people want to eat by themselves. I don't have anything against that. But it was just the way he was studying people that kind of creeped me out. To top it off, he ordered an appetizer, a meal, and a dessert. Then he didn't bother to leave me a tip."

"What did he look like?" Natalie asked.

Mandy shrugged. "Nothing outstanding. Dark clothing." She shrugged again. "I don't know. He was nothing remarkable."

Maybe that was the way this guy wanted to look. He fit the description of the man Jim had described. That couldn't be a coincidence...could it?

Natalie turned back to Mandy. "Did you see my sister interact with him at all?"

Mandy thought about it a moment before shaking her head. "No, he was seated in my section. He probably left about ten minutes before my shift ended. I didn't see him in the parking lot either."

Natalie thanked the waitress. She wasn't sure if that lead would take them anywhere or not. But the more information she had, the better.

"There is one more thing." Mandy shifted, in no hurry to leave. "Lexi *did* make an offhanded comment to me two days ago. She said she felt like someone has been watching her lately, but she never could pinpoint who it might be. It just left her feeling a little off balance."

A chill washed over Natalie.

What if somebody had been watching Lexi? And then abducted her?

Natalie could hardly stomach the thought.

TWELVE

Andrew didn't like where this was going.

Could there be two separate crimes going on here?

He didn't think so. But the whole thing was just strange. Because why would a man who'd tried to kill Natalie back in Cincinnati come down here and abduct her sister?

It just didn't make sense.

"What if somebody thought Lexi was me?"

Natalie's question startled him. "What?"

"I know it might sound crazy. But when Lexi and I were younger, people used to mistake us for twins. We shared a lot of the same traits. She bleached her hair and gave herself a different cut when she got old enough. But maybe someone who didn't know us might think that I was trying to change my identity and—"

"And that you had essentially become Lexi." Andrew paused and chewed on that thought a moment. "So someone could think you left Cincinnati and came here to start over."

"If this guy who wants me dead took Lexi instead, then why does he still have her? Certainly, he knows by now that she isn't me. What's he going to do with her?" Natalie's voice sounded strained.

"That's a good question. At this point, he has to realize you're not the same person." Andrew absently swirled his straw in his ice water. "Then what about the person who came to the cabin? How does that match?"

"I thought someone was outside the cabin at about 4:00 a.m. So what if this guy grabbed Lexi as she left work, realized it wasn't her, and then went to the cabin to see if I was there. But then I ran into you and Rambo, so he wasn't able to get me."

"And now he's holding Lexi as collateral."

Natalie's face went a little paler. "Yes, exactly. There's so much to think about."

Before they could talk about it anymore, their food came.

Andrew lifted a prayer before digging in.

He noticed Natalie watching him and asked, "You don't pray before you eat?"

She shrugged. "I used to. And I'm starting again. I guess I got wrapped up in the busyness of my life, and I kind of let my relationship with God take a back seat to everything. But I'm beginning to realize what a huge mistake that was. Without God in my life, I feel like a ship without a rudder, you know?"

"Yeah, I totally know." Andrew did understand.

The revelation made him feel a little closer to Natalie, to know that they both were believers.

He ate his sandwich and chewed on his thoughts as he did.

There was a lot to comprehend here.

He wanted to trust Natalie. To believe that she was telling him the truth.

But then again, he'd trusted Sarah. He'd even proposed to her, and she'd said yes.

He'd been prepared to spend the rest of his life with her.

Then she'd stabbed him in the back.

The pain had been brutal. Looking back, Andrew could

see some red flags he'd ignored. Her disregard for some people and her adoration of others.

It all depended on who could provide her with what she wanted at the time.

But Andrew hadn't seen it. He'd been blind to it.

Sarah had broken his heart.

Even though he'd learned his lesson, that fact made it hard for Andrew to trust any woman.

Even Natalie.

They both remained quiet as they ate, and after they finished their food, Andrew paid the bill—again.

"I can pay—" Natalie started.

"I know you can. But I'd like to do this for you. I'm guessing there haven't been many people in your life lately that have had your back. Am I right?"

Andrew could see the truth in her eyes.

She hadn't.

Slowly, she nodded and smiled. "Thank you. Again. Maybe I could make dinner for us one night, after all this is over."

Andrew's gut clenched. He liked that idea. Maybe a little bit too much. "That would be nice."

Before he could think any more about it, Frank walked in from the back of the kitchen.

They were right on time.

It was three o'clock, and now it was time to meet with the manager.

But as Andrew rose to walk over to Frank, another restaurant patron caught his eye.

Detective Caruso.

The man was seated at the bar in the distance, and he didn't try to hide the fact that he was watching them. He even waved and smirked.

Andrew's muscles bristled.

What exactly was the deal with this guy?

* * *

Natalie sat in an office off the restaurant's kitchen and stared at a computer screen showing the recorded video footage. Andrew stood behind her and just to her left. Frank sat to her right in another chair. And Rambo paced in between them all, getting head rubs wherever he could.

Frank rested his hand on the computer's mouse and scrolled, trying to find the time Lexi left.

Anxiety thrummed inside Natalie.

She needed answers. Yet, at the same time, she feared what she might find out.

What if she witnessed something awful happen to Lexi? She would never scrub those images from her mind.

Just like the dinner party.

Maybe she should let Andrew watch this first.

But she needed to know firsthand. She needed to see this for herself.

There was so much she'd like to say to Lexi. What if she didn't get the chance?

No, she couldn't think that way. This was her sister. Natalie would find her.

She had to.

She'd always hoped that she and Lexi would find some common ground. That they could be close again like they were when they were kids.

With Mom having started a new life and Dad passing away after a heart attack last year, Natalie and Lexi were all each other had. Part of Natalie had hoped that if she came here, the two would get past some of the barriers erected between them.

But now it didn't look like that would happen.

At least not until Natalie found her sister.

Nausea gurgled inside her.

"Here it is." Frank slowed the video to regular time and hit Play.

She watched the screen and saw Lexi on the black-and-white footage as she left the restaurant. It was dark outside and hard to make out many details. Only a few vehicles were parked behind the restaurant—most of them belonging to employees, she had to assume.

Lexi, with her blonde hair cut in that sharp wedge and her large hoop earrings, walked toward her car.

Natalie sucked in a breath. The earrings. They matched the one she'd found in the stream. Lexi had been back there, exactly where Rambo had led them.

Natalie continued watching as Lexi pulled her purse up higher on her shoulder and strolled along as if she didn't have a care in the world.

She'd always been street-smart. She'd learned some lessons the hard way after she got involved with the wrong crowd in high school.

Natalie knew even though Lexi appeared aloof, she was always alert to her surroundings.

Natalie could hardly breathe as she continued watching.

Andrew seemed to sense that, and he squeezed her shoulder reassuringly. His touch seemed to bring her back down to earth, and she released the air from her lungs.

She could do this.

She had no other choice at this point.

Lexi reached her car and pulled her keys from her pocketbook.

Something had to happen soon. But what? What could've possibly kept Lexi from driving away?

Natalie leaned closer, more curious than ever to see what happened.

Lexi jammed her key into the door and then opened it. But, before she climbed inside, she paused.

She glanced at the woods in the distance as if she'd heard something.

The security camera footage had no sound, so Natalie could only guess what that might have been.

Could someone have called for her? Cried for help?

It was impossible to know for certain.

On the screen, Lexi glanced around. Then she stepped back from her car, hit the lock and slammed the door.

She took a tentative step toward the woods and paused.

After a few seconds, she raked a hand through her hair and looked around again.

It seemed certain that she was hearing something. Natalie could only guess what that might be, though.

Several seconds later, with one more glance behind her, Lexi disappeared into the woods.

Natalie watched several more minutes of the video, but Lexi never reappeared.

Rambo had led them through the woods to the other parking lot, where he'd lost the scent.

That must have been where someone had taken Lexi. Maybe this person had forced her through the woods and into his car.

It would have to be someone who'd planned ahead. Someone who knew her routines. Who knew what time she got off work.

Someone who knew that in the dead of night, there would be no one to pay attention and see what was happening.

Anger roiled inside Natalie.

Someone had tricked her sister. Lured her out into those woods.

And now Natalie had no idea where Lexi might be or how to find her.

Frank offered Natalie a cold soda, and the two walked into the kitchen. Andrew knew she could use a breather, but he wanted to see the rest of the video.

He sat in the chair Natalie had been in and fast-forwarded the video. There had to be an explanation for how Lexi's phone had gotten smashed and thrown under the car.

Three hours after Lexi walked into the woods, a man appeared from the shadows. It was too dark to tell anything about him.

But he went to Lexi's car. Opened the door. Did something inside—probably destroyed the cushions.

It was too dark and grainy to tell if he'd dropped her cell phone beneath the car. But it had to have been him. Nothing else made sense.

When he was done, he walked away as if nothing had happened.

There was no sign of Lexi.

He called Natalie and Frank back into the office and showed them what he'd found.

"What does this mean? Do you think…" Natalie's voice trailed off as if she couldn't finish the thought.

A bad feeling gurgled in his gut, and he could only imagine what Natalie was feeling.

"We don't know what it means. This guy could've taken her somewhere. He could still have her." Andrew wasn't sure his theory was solid, but it was the best he could come up with given the circumstances.

Andrew asked for a copy of the video to be sent to his email, and Frank said he would send it over right away. He said he'd also send a copy to the police if they needed that, and Andrew encouraged him to do so. But he told Frank not to send it to Detective Caruso.

Frank gave him an odd look but didn't question him.

Andrew wasn't sure if he could trust Caruso yet. The detective wasn't necessarily a suspect, but he was definitely someone to be cautious around.

Even though it made sense that the person who'd taken

Lexi would be the same person who had tried to kill Natalie, Andrew needed to be sure.

Because if two people were involved, then Detective Caruso would be one of his top suspects.

Andrew, Natalie and Rambo left the restaurant and paused in the parking lot, which was beginning to fill up with the evening crowd.

He turned toward Natalie. "I don't think there's anything else we can do here."

A frown tugged at her lips. "It doesn't seem right just to go back to the cabin and do nothing."

"Maybe we should regroup. We've done a lot here today, and I know you've got to be tired. I know you didn't sleep much last night."

She stared at him a moment before finally nodding. "Okay then. Let's get back."

But Andrew knew she didn't want to leave. He couldn't blame her. If he were in her shoes, he'd want to stay here and continue looking also.

They went back to his Bronco, and he put Rambo in the back seat just as before. Then he and Natalie climbed in, and they took off back to the cabin.

The sun would be setting soon, and the sky was already growing gray.

He could only imagine the nightmare Natalie was going through and the things that she was wrestling with. He wished he could ease some of her worries. But he knew there was no hope of that happening right now.

Instead, he remained quiet and gave her space to process everything that they had learned.

It didn't take long to weave through traffic and pull back up to Natalie's cabin.

As he stared at the small structure in front of them, he turned to Natalie. "If it's okay with you, I need to check this out first. I'd feel better."

She nodded stiffly and handed him her house key.

He opened his door before looking back at her. "I'll leave Rambo with you. Lock the doors after I get out. Just in case. And I'm leaving the keys in the truck, so…"

He didn't have to finish his statement. He could see realization washing over her.

Andrew hated to scare her. It wasn't his intention. But he had to be smart right now.

He stepped into the cabin and glanced around the living room.

From what he remembered from when he'd been in here earlier, everything looked as if it was in place.

But his main concern was making sure no one else was inside. No one was hiding anywhere.

Andrew searched the living room and the kitchen. Nothing.

Then he moved to the bathroom and the closet.

Again, there was nothing.

He opened the door to Lexi's room and checked it out. The space was clear. Even if someone had been in this room, they could have tossed it and Andrew wouldn't have been able to tell. It was so messy and disorganized.

He was still amazed at how different the two sisters were.

Then he opened the door to Natalie's room. He glanced around, looking for anything that could be out of place.

Everything looked okay. Except…

His gaze stopped on the mirror.

A message had been written there in red lipstick.

This is all your fault.

THIRTEEN

As soon as Natalie saw Andrew step out of the cabin, she knew something was wrong. His shoulders were too stiff and his walk too fast.

Her lungs squeezed as she anticipated the worst.

What if he'd found Lexi?

No, Natalie couldn't think like that.

At the same time, she couldn't stop doing so.

She licked her lips as soon as he climbed back into the truck. "Well?"

The look he gave her wasn't reassuring. "Someone's been in there."

Her hand pressed against her heart. "How do you know? What happened?"

"Someone left you a message." He pulled out his phone and showed her a picture of it.

She gasped as she read the words. *This is all your fault.*

"Is that written in...blood?" In Natalie's mind, she knew it didn't exactly look like blood, but the red was still jarring.

"Probably lipstick," Andrew said. "Either way, it's not safe for you to stay here."

Her chest tightened even more. "I have nowhere else to go. I mean, I guess I could find a hotel, but..."

"Look, I know we just met, and I know it's probably a

strange offer to make. But why don't you stay at my place? I have an extra bedroom."

"I couldn't do that…"

"I'd feel a lot better if you weren't alone. If you had someone to keep an eye on you."

Her thoughts raced. "But how do we know that he won't find us there?"

"I suppose we don't. But if he does, I'll be there to protect you. Rambo too."

She looked over her shoulder at the dog. He sat there, tail wagging, and if Natalie didn't know better, she'd think he was smiling.

Her heart pounded harder. "Again, I can't ask you to do that. You don't even know me. You've already done so much…"

"I know I don't know you, even though part of me feels like I do."

His statement caused her to suck in a breath.

Natalie had felt that today also. She hadn't wanted to give that thought any notice. But the realization had been there.

The two of them had an easy connection. When Natalie talked to Andrew, she felt as if she'd known him for much longer than she actually had.

The thought of him protecting her, on one hand, made her uneasy—because she truly didn't want to make him go out of his way. But on the other hand, his presence brought her immense comfort.

"If anyone comes near the cabin, Rambo will alert us," he continued. "I *am* a trained law enforcement officer. I know how to handle myself in these situations."

His words sounded so reassuring. So tempting.

But did she really want to rely on someone she'd just met?

She wasn't sure.

"I can't make you." Andrew shifted to look her in the eyes. "The last thing I want is for you to be uncomfortable. I can follow you into town, and you can see if you can find a hotel room. I did hear that everything is booked, however. There's a big Southern gospel music festival starting tomorrow."

She *had* heard something about that. He was right—finding another place to stay would be difficult.

"If it wasn't for my sister, I would get out of this town altogether," she said with a sigh. "But I can't leave while she's missing."

"And someone is probably banking on that."

Natalie thought about it another moment before nodding and releasing a slow breath. "Okay then. I'll stay at your place. Thank you. Can I grab a few of my things inside first?"

"Of course. I'll go with you—just to be on the safe side."

Natalie realized at this very moment that Andrew was truly a gift from God. Because she wasn't sure if she would have been able to get this far today without him by her side.

Andrew checked out his place just to be certain before he let Natalie and Rambo inside.

Everything appeared clear. But he was still on edge after everything that had happened.

Rambo sniffed around the living room, then headed for the kitchen as was his usual routine. He liked to look for crumbs that may have fallen onto the floor—not one to miss an opportunity for a taste of human food, no matter how small. But when he got near the door leading out to the backyard, he sniffed harder.

"What are you doing, boy? You were just outside. You're staying in."

Instead of going to the living room to lie down in his dog bed, he parked himself right there by the back door.

Just as a precaution, Andrew looked through the window but didn't see anything.

Maybe Rambo had caught a whiff of an animal outside. One time he went ballistic when a raccoon got into the trash can.

But finally, the dog settled down.

Once he was sure Rambo wasn't going to get into any mischief, Andrew watched Natalie soak in his place. She'd been here earlier but had probably been too distracted with everything else to notice any details.

He hadn't made very many changes since he moved here, and it mostly looked like his grandparents had left it.

Thankfully, they'd had simple tastes and had decorated with warm rugs, brown leather couches, and other typical cabin decor—a small bear carving by the river stone fireplace, scenic pictures of the mountains on the walls. Really, Andrew felt like he was home every time he was here.

"Let me just get Rambo some water and something to eat." He stepped toward the kitchen. "Make yourself comfortable."

Natalie nodded and sat on the couch, looking rather stiff.

Andrew couldn't blame her in the situation. He knew it wasn't ideal, but he would try to make her feel at ease the best he could.

In the kitchen, Andrew fed and watered Rambo before turning back to Natalie. "Can I get you anything?"

She shook her head. "I'm okay."

Andrew came back into the living room and started a fire.

There was only a slight chill in the air, but there was also something he'd always found very comforting about a fire. He hoped Natalie might find some comfort in the warm flames also.

Once it was blazing, he wandered back into the kitchen. He wasn't hungry. Breakfast and lunch had filled him up.

But something warm sounded nice.

"Would you like me to fix you some tea?" he asked.

"I'd love some."

He kept a tin of loose-leaf peppermint tea in his cupboard. He put the kettle on and waited for it to whistle.

Then he poured two cups, one for him and one for Natalie, and took them to the coffee table. He sat a comfortable distance away from her on the couch, ready to relax and stretch out for a bit.

"Should we tell Caruso about the message in the cabin?" Natalie asked.

She'd obviously been thinking about everything as he worked.

"Yes, but we can call him in a minute." He stared at her as they waited for the tea to cool off. "I thought maybe you might need to talk first."

"I'm not sure what else there is to say." Natalie shrugged. "It was bad enough to be running for my life. But now my sister has been pulled into this."

Just as earlier, Andrew had to resist the urge to reach out and touch her, to offer some type of comfort.

Instead, he nodded. "I can only imagine what you're going through, and I'm sorry."

She shook her head, appearing lost in her own thoughts. "I don't even know what to do next. Do I keep looking for her? Is this guy going to be in touch with me about the fact that he has her? Or is the best-case scenario that maybe my sister will just show up again, and I'll realize all this was a misunderstanding? Maybe there's some innocent, logical explanation for all this that we haven't thought of yet."

Andrew knew that was wishful thinking on her part, but he didn't voice his thoughts about it. She was still coming to terms with all that had happened. Instead, he said,

"Maybe we can come up with a plan for all those scenarios. I know that Detective Caruso said we needed to wait forty-eight hours—"

"But it sounds like he has a beef with Lexi since she rejected him. She doesn't always handle things in a considerate manner."

Andrew rubbed his jaw. "It was rather obvious he has a personal issue with her. That doesn't bode well. I'd hope he's objective enough not to let that cloud his judgment, but I can't say that for sure."

"So if the local police aren't going to help, do I keep looking?" Natalie turned toward him, making no secret of the fact that she was watching for his reaction.

"There's nothing wrong with trying to find out more answers. But right now, we don't have very much to go on. We know Lexi left work, then went into the woods and headed for the stream. That was the last trace of her scent Rambo could pick up on. We know there was a man in the restaurant who was potentially watching her."

"And who came back later to rifle through her car."

"Yes," Andrew said. "Then someone was at the cabin in the middle of the night, they sent me that text, and they left that message written in lipstick at Lexi's cabin. And don't forget about the man I chased down the street today. He had to be running for some reason. This person…he isn't backing off, and he's making no secret of it."

Natalie sighed and leaned back. "The person who took her clearly wants to send a message."

"Yes, they do. Don't forget someone tried to run us off the mountain road."

"How could I forget? That was a close call. Too close. But how does it all fit together?" As the fire heated the room, she pushed up her sleeves.

When she did, Andrew caught a glimpse of the scars there and sucked in a breath.

The mark on her jaw was nothing compared to the ones on her arms.

Natalie seemed to notice him staring and quickly pushed her sleeves down.

Regret filled him. "I didn't mean to make you uncomfortable. I'm sorry."

"I know they're not pretty." She rubbed her arms self-consciously.

"I just wasn't expecting…so much."

She shrugged, clearly unnerved. "Like I said, the attack was brutal."

More understanding filled Andrew. He wished he hadn't stared. Wished they hadn't had this conversation.

He hated the pain on Natalie's face right now.

"For what it's worth, you're a very attractive woman. The scars don't change that." Andrew hadn't meant to say the words. But he had. And they were true. Natalie was a beautiful woman. Inside and out.

She blushed a little, but keeping her composure, she lifted her tea, blew on it, then took a sip.

"What do you think?" he asked. "I got it at a shop in town."

"It's good. I didn't see you as a tea kind of guy," Natalie murmured, a glimmer of curiosity in her gaze.

"No? What kind of guy did you see me as?"

"A coffee drinker. No sugar. No cream. Straight up black coffee."

He shrugged. "I enjoy coffee too, but my mom is British. She taught me the fine art of drinking tea."

"Did she teach you how to make scones as well?"

"Of course, and homemade jam to spread on top."

"Fancy." Natalie started to nod when she touched her throat and then shot up straight and started coughing.

Andrew straightened. What was wrong?

Was Natalie choking…on tea?

She opened her mouth as if she wanted to spit. Instead, she made almost a gagging sound.

She set down her teacup and began to look around frantically.

She needed her EpiPen, Andrew realized.

Something in the tea had triggered her allergy.

Natalie felt her throat closing.

She needed help, and she needed it now.

She glanced around the cabin, searching for her purse.

But Andrew beat her to it.

He grabbed it from behind the couch and rifled through it until he found the EpiPen. Then he rushed back to her, uncapped the end and jabbed the needle into her leg.

Natalie waited, desperate for breath. The edges of her consciousness blurred.

She just needed to breathe.

Only seconds later, the EpiPen kicked in, and she gasped in lifesaving oxygen.

She sucked air into her lungs. Then more. Then more.

Natalie's limbs trembled again as the medication continued to ease her symptoms.

She'd come close to death, hadn't she?

Again.

What was going to happen next?

She didn't even want to know.

Andrew sat close, carefully observing her and ready to act if necessary. "I should take you to the hospital."

Natalie shook her head in a way that didn't leave room for questions, although she continued to draw in raspy breaths.

"Your symptoms are subsiding enough?" he asked.

She nodded. "I'll be okay. This has happened before. I'll be fine."

Andrew gave her another moment to compose herself. But she saw the questions in his gaze.

"Can I see the container the tea came in?" she finally asked.

"Of course." Andrew went to the kitchen and brought the tin back. "But I don't think there are any nuts in there."

"You'd be surprised what you can find peanuts in," Natalie said, her voice scratchy as she reviewed the ingredients listed on the label. "Just peppermint. No peanuts. And it doesn't say anything about being processed in a facility that has peanuts, or even any kind of tree nuts. This should be safe for me."

"I don't even have any peanut butter here. Could it be something you ate at the restaurant? Maybe a delayed reaction?"

"No, my allergic reactions come on almost immediately."

Andrew held out his hand. "May I?"

She handed the tea canister back to him as she continued to try to focus on her breathing before panic hit her on top of the allergy event.

Andrew stepped back from her and opened the container again and poured some of the tea leaves into his hand.

Then Natalie saw him frown.

"What is it?" She didn't have the energy to get up and look closer.

"Something that looks like specks of peanut dust are covering the tea leaves."

"What?" Natalie watched him sniff the leaves. "What are you thinking?"

"My theory is going to sound crazy."

"Share it anyway."

Andrew's gaze met hers. "What if someone knew you

had a peanut allergy, broke in here and put that dust in the tea?"

"They'd also have to know I like to drink tea."

"And that you'd be here with me to drink it." He frowned and rubbed a hand over his face.

"That's a lot of uncertainties, isn't it?"

"It is. But the way things have been going, I wouldn't put it past this guy to try this." He glanced at his cupboard. "I'll check some other food items, but it wouldn't surprise me if there's peanut dust there also."

Natalie shivered at the thought.

"Rambo was acting a little peculiar once we walked inside, but I figured he had smelled an animal nearby or something." Andrew rubbed his dog's head as he frowned.

"I didn't even notice." Natalie drew her knees to her chest. "How would someone even know that I have a peanut allergy? It's not as if I advertise it."

"But in both of the restaurants we were in today, you did mention that to the waitress. So if anyone was close enough, they could have heard. I'm assuming you probably have that conversation wherever you go to eat."

"I do. I suppose you're right. Someone could have been listening in." Natalie rubbed her arms, which trembled with adrenaline. "I'm glad you were here. Thank you."

Andrew glanced around, his expression still tense. "I don't like the idea that someone was in my cabin."

"He was in mine too. Maybe this person has been watching us all day and left that message, assuming I might come back over here to stay with you. That's the only thing that really makes sense."

"You're right. Someone has put a lot of thought into planning this. I don't like this. I'm going to need to take a second look at everything. And, of course, you can't eat any food that's already open, just in case it's been tampered with. Only sealed packages."

Natalie nodded, trying not to let on how bad she felt. Her adrenaline burst was quickly fading, but sweat still covered her forehead and dizziness made her lightheaded. Soon, exhaustion would hit.

Still, she was recovering.

She knew what it was like after using the EpiPen. She'd had to use it three other times in her life. It was lifesaving but not fun.

But it would be a long time before Natalie felt at ease.

If she couldn't even let her guard down long enough to have a simple cup of tea, how long would it be before she could stop looking over her shoulder?

FOURTEEN

Andrew and Natalie talked a while longer before Natalie said she was tired and wanted to get some rest.

Once she was safely settled in his spare bedroom, Andrew went back to the living room and grabbed his computer. He wanted to check the security camera footage from today.

If someone had been in his cabin, his cameras should have picked up on it.

He watched carefully, anxious to see what he might discover.

But for the first several hours, there was nothing.

With a sigh, he leaned back and rubbed his eyes.

This wasn't the fun part about being a detective. TV made it look glamorous. But the truth was, sometimes finding answers required a lot of tedious tasks—like stake-outs and hours of watching videos where nothing happens.

Finally, movement on the camera by the back door caught his eye.

A shadow appeared on the right side of the screen, coming out from the woods.

He held his breath as he waited to see a face. But instead of seeing that, a gloved hand appeared on the screen.

What…?

A moment later, spray paint covered the camera lens, and it went black.

Anger burned through him.

Andrew had more than one camera, but that was the only one that had picked up anything. The man had carefully avoided the others. This guy knew what he was doing. He'd taken out the one he needed to—effectively concealing any traces of his identity.

They were dealing with someone who was smart and cunning.

The fact left him feeling on edge.

He also wanted to research the incident that had happened to Natalie back in Cincinnati a little bit more for himself.

He vaguely remembered hearing something about it on the news, but he hadn't been paying careful attention.

Several news articles popped up—actually, more than he could count.

This had definitely made the national news. There were not only articles, but TV specials on it.

He braced himself for whatever he was about to learn. Had Natalie been interviewed?

He scanned several clips but didn't see her face. Articles simply called her an unnamed surviving victim.

But there were several blurred-out images of the crime scene. Even with the filters in place, the scene was still grisly. Even as a seasoned cop, Andrew had trouble imagining what had gone down there. It was no wonder Natalie was having such a hard time.

But why would a killer who'd planned on a mass shooting bring his dog with him? He couldn't help but ask himself that question. It was risky, and having an animal with him would make everything more complicated.

So what sense did it make?

He wasn't sure.

On a whim, Andrew grabbed his phone and called one of his former colleagues who was now working in Cincinnati. Maybe he should have asked Natalie first, but he didn't think she'd mind.

Andrew wanted some insight on what had happened, things beyond what the news may have reported.

Chief Grayson Denning answered on the second ring. "Hey, man. Long time, no see."

"Yes, it has been a long time."

They caught up for a few moments before Andrew got to his point.

"Look, this is a long story, but I may have found a possible connection with the case that happened in Cincinnati a few months ago, the one where the executives were gunned down in one of their homes."

Grayson made a clicking sound with his tongue. "That one. That case still haunts me. All of us really. I've been doing this for a long time, and that was one of the worst scenes I've ever walked into."

"I can only imagine. I'm not sure how much you're at liberty to share, but I wondered if you had any suspects."

Grayson let out a breath. "Our most likely suspect is a man by the name of Daniel Lumberton. He's the former boyfriend of Jennifer Hardwood, one of the executives who was at the house. They'd had a nasty breakup the week before, and he had vowed revenge."

"So you think he showed up at this party and gunned everyone down?"

"Apparently, he was on some medications that gave him poor impulse control. And he did have a dog also. A German shepherd."

"Where is this guy now?" Andrew asked.

"He's in the wind. After the murders, we went to bring him in, and he was gone. No one has seen or heard from him since."

"I'm assuming your guys are still looking for him?"

"We are. I've had a trace on his cell phone and his credit cards, but there's been nothing. The guy may be a little off, but he's also brilliant. He knows how to disappear."

"Is he your only suspect?"

Grayson let out another long breath as if thinking about it. "He's our *best* suspect. There were no other credible threats against Drexel. Daniel makes the most sense *and* he disappeared." Grayson paused. "So why are you asking all this?"

Andrew stared down the hallway at Natalie's door before saying, "I actually ran into the only survivor."

"Natalie?" He let out a whistle. "The things that woman has been through... She's a real warrior. She was at the peak of her career when this happened, and now people are worried about whether she'll ever truly recover. How *is* she doing?"

"She's shaken up, as you can imagine."

"Where are you right now?"

Andrew glanced around his cabin and frowned. "I'd rather not say just because she'd like her privacy."

"Understandable. But really, disappearing was the best thing she could do. After that guy showed up at her condo, we offered her police protection. She didn't want it. Instead, she said she was leaving town. Honestly, I figured that was the best thing she could do anyway."

"Good to know. I'm going to do whatever I can to figure out what's going on here. But I'm worried this guy may have found her here."

Grayson grunted. "If that's the case, then you need to be very careful. Because I'm pretty sure this guy doesn't have a conscience."

As Andrew ended the call, a hollow feeling dipped in his gut.

He didn't like the sound of any of this.

Before he could think about it for too long, Rambo suddenly stood, his fur standing on end.

The dog stared at the door, and a low growl escaped his throat.

Andrew rose to his feet and grabbed the gun holstered at his waist.

Rambo's reaction could only mean one thing.

Someone was outside.

Had the killer come back to finish what he'd started?

Something jerked Natalie from her sleep.

She sat up in bed, and sweat covered her skin as her heart pounded out of control.

It took her a moment to realize where she was.

Andrew's cabin. She'd gone to lie down for a while in his spare bedroom and must have fallen asleep.

How long had she been out?

What was that noise?

She paused, listening for the sound again.

But it was gone.

She'd *definitely* heard something. A dog bark maybe. A door opening?

Her heart pounded even faster.

Was it Andrew? Or had someone else stopped by the cabin?

She didn't know.

Should she peek out the door?

But what if it was the man in black? What if he'd somehow taken Andrew and Rambo out of the picture?

She wished she still had her knife.

She didn't know what to do.

Part of her wanted to hide under the covers and simply pretend like she hadn't heard anything.

But that could end with her death—or maybe even Andrew's.

Finding her courage, she tugged on a sweatshirt and slipped on her sneakers. Then she walked to the bedroom door and listened.

She stood there for a moment, trembling claiming her yet again.

Natalie had never known what it was truly like to be scared until recently. Now she couldn't seem to shake her fear. It popped up all the time, even when it wasn't warranted.

But right now, she felt for sure her feelings were justified.

After staring at the door a moment and contemplating what she wanted to do, Natalie finally twisted the door handle and cracked it open.

She saw a figure charging toward her and gasped. She threw herself back, fearing the worst.

Until Andrew's face came into view.

But his expression brought another wave of terror surging through her.

"Rambo heard something outside," he rushed out. "I'm going to go check it out."

Without thinking, Natalie grabbed his arm. "Maybe you shouldn't do that."

He gripped his gun. "I'll be careful. I promise. And I'll leave Rambo in here with you."

Natalie glanced at the dog, who'd followed behind him.

She wasn't sure if being alone with the canine brought her comfort or not.

But so far, Rambo had only been gentle and kind around her.

She forced herself to nod.

Andrew instructed Rambo to stay in the bedroom with her.

Then Andrew turned to Natalie. "Lock the door behind me and only open it for me. Do you understand?"

She nodded, feeling half numb and half panicked.

"Do you have your cell phone?" he asked. "Because if I'm not back in five minutes, I want you to call the police. Not for my sake, but for yours."

Another shot of terror went through her.

Why was this happening? It was like a never-ending nightmare.

Andrew gave her one more glance before stepping from her room.

When he was gone, Natalie called Rambo to the bed.

The dog jumped onto the mattress beside her, and Natalie began to stroke his head.

Having the animal so close brought her a strange comfort—a comfort that surprised her.

The dog was obviously on guard. If he heard anything, he'd alert her.

Not all dogs were like the one that had attacked her.

Just like not all men were like Philip.

She'd have to work to try to remember that fact.

Natalie waited as the minutes seemed to drag by.

What was going on outside? Was Andrew okay?

What if whoever was out there was simply waiting for him to open the front door so he could shoot him?

Natalie's gut tightened at the thought of that.

But she would have heard the gunfire if that was the case.

At that thought, a yell sounded outside.

Was that Andrew?

She couldn't tell. The sound was muffled from here.

Her heart pounded so loudly that its beats were all she could hear.

She gripped Rambo and leaned closer to the dog, burying her face in his fur.

Then she began to lift up fervent prayers.

* * *

Andrew was careful not to be seen.

Since he didn't know who was out here or what kind of weapons they might have, he needed to use something as a shield.

That's why he leaned into a hickory tree.

Then he waited for any more telltale sounds.

Someone was definitely out here.

Rambo had confirmed that for him.

But Andrew sensed it also.

He felt danger closing in.

He'd briefly wondered if maybe it could be one of the black bears who frequented this area.

But he didn't think so.

Not during the winter months.

Either way, there were dangers out here and he needed to be on guard.

He listened, knowing that the trespasser would need to make a move eventually. Andrew had learned to be very patient from all the stakeouts he'd been on.

He could stay in this position for hours if he had to.

Finally, he heard another stick crack.

That was him.

The person was probably only twelve feet away if Andrew had to guess. Farther up the hill toward the north.

Moving carefully, Andrew moved to another tree. Then another. All in an effort to get closer and see who this person was and what they were up to.

The one thing he couldn't let the trespasser do was get inside his cabin—get to Natalie.

Andrew had probably left the house three minutes ago. That meant he had two minutes to figure out what was going on or Natalie would call the police.

Her safety was his main concern.

Carefully, Andrew moved behind another tree, thankful

the moon wasn't out tonight. The black sky offered him the cover of darkness.

As he peered around the tree, he spotted a dark figure dressed in black. Whoever it was, the man was staring at the house right now.

Who *was* that?

The man wore a hat, which made it hard to make out any of his features.

But now was the moment of truth.

Andrew needed to put an end to all of this.

He stepped out from behind the tree and raised his gun. "Put your hands up or I'll shoot."

Then he waited for the man's next move.

FIFTEEN

Andrew's eyes widened at the familiar figure who stepped out.

"Dylan?" Andrew muttered.

The cook raised his hands, a look of terror on his face. "Don't shoot me. Please. I'm not trying to hurt anybody."

Andrew remained bristled. "Then what are you doing here?"

"I'm looking for Lexi."

"You think she's here at my place?"

"I don't know where she is."

Andrew wasn't sure he was buying this guy's story. "Leave your hands up."

Dylan did as he was instructed.

Andrew slid his gun back into its holster and then patted him down.

He didn't have any weapons.

Knowing that, Andrew took the guy's arm and led him back to the cabin. "You and I need to talk."

Dylan was now a prime suspect. The man could have learned that Natalie had a peanut allergy. He'd been in the restaurant, and he was friends with the waitresses. Plus, he knew where Andrew lived.

He didn't trust this guy.

But he was going to find out some answers.

He led Dylan into the cabin and pushed him onto the couch. Then he called down the hallway for Natalie to come out.

A moment later, her door opened, and Rambo bounded toward him.

The canine growled when he saw Dylan, and the man's eyes widened with fright.

Good. Andrew wanted this guy to be on edge.

But Andrew called Rambo off.

A few moments later, Natalie hesitantly stepped out, her eyes wary.

"Is everything okay?" Her words ran together. Then her gaze fell on the couch, and she gasped. "Dylan?"

He ran a hand through his hair and shrugged. "It's a long story."

Natalie came to stand beside Andrew, seeming to find some comfort in his presence.

But she didn't say anything else. She just waited.

"Did you take Lexi?" Andrew demanded.

"Take Lexi?" Dylan's eyes widened. "Where?"

"Did you take her somewhere against her will?"

"No. Why would I do that?"

"She's missing, and you're here right now."

He shook his head quickly and adamantly. "It's like I told you. I'm only here because I'm looking for her, not because I did anything to her."

Andrew still wasn't sure he was buying this guy's story. "You need to tell us everything that you know."

"I don't know much." He shrugged, looking frazzled and out of sorts.

"You obviously knew something that led you here tonight. Why would you even think to come to my house?"

"I've been watching you guys today," he rushed. "I thought you might know something. Then I went to Lexi's place, just to see if she was there or not. She wasn't."

"How did that lead you here?" Andrew demanded.

"As I was driving past, I saw the lights on over at this place and it just made me wonder...so I thought I'd come and check it out. And I saw the two of you inside and when you came out, I knew I'd been caught. That's the reason that I hid."

"Are you sure there's not any more to the story?" Andrew demanded.

"I promise you. There's nothing else. I'm worried, just like you are."

"What aren't you telling us?" Andrew leaned closer.

"Lexi didn't want me talking about it."

Natalie bristled. "About what?"

"About the reason she picked the cabin out here to live in instead of staying in town."

"Why did she pick that cabin? It doesn't seem like her."

"She said she needed to stay somewhere private," Dylan said. "She had a side job that made her good money."

Andrew crossed his arms. "What kind of side job?"

"She...she didn't tell me."

"Is that the truth?"

Dylan nodded quickly. "Yes, I promise it is. But I suspect that whatever she's been doing is illegal."

SIXTEEN

Natalie woke up the next morning after another restless night.

At least she'd managed to drift off and get a few hours of sleep. Maybe that little bit of rest would help her think more clearly.

She hoped today might provide some of the answers she desperately sought.

Every time she closed her eyes last night, she imagined Lexi and what she might be going through. Then Natalie felt guilty to be enjoying a warm bed and the safety of Andrew's home while she didn't know what was happening with her sister.

With a frown, she dragged herself out of bed. The air around her was cool, but she thought she caught the aroma of a cozy fire in the other room. A real wood fire wasn't something she was used to. She'd had a gas fireplace in Cincinnati. But she preferred the scents of burning wood over the smell of a natural gas fireplace.

If she wasn't careful, she could get used to waking up to the comfort of the fire and… Was that coffee she smelled brewing?

She quickly grabbed a few things from her overnight bag before slipping into the bathroom across the hall to get ready.

When she emerged after a quick shower, she dried her hair and got dressed. After quickly applying a little makeup, she stepped out of the bathroom and noticed a new scent filled the air.

She sniffed. Was that bacon?

She followed her nose into the kitchen where she spotted Andrew standing behind the griddle.

He offered her a tentative smile as he raised his tongs in greeting. "Good morning."

He flashed a smile that almost made Natalie feel normal a moment. The feeling was nice but gone entirely too quickly.

"I thought you might be hungry," he continued.

"I am. Anything I can do to help?"

"I've got this. Have a seat. How did you sleep last night?"

"I managed to get a few hours in." Natalie settled at the breakfast bar and watched him as he cooked some pancakes and bacon. "It smells great in here."

"Everything I'm cooking is from unopened packages."

A sense of relief filled her. Natalie had felt a flash of worry when she'd remembered the peanut dust from last night.

Someone clearly wanted to hurt her and was determined to do so using whatever means possible. She had to remain on guard.

"Do you often cook breakfast? Or do you usually grab cereal or fruit and yogurt?" Natalie didn't know why she was asking, but she was curious.

"I like a variety. I suppose it depends on the day, what I'm in the mood for. How about you?" He flipped the bacon and scraped some of the grease off the griddle.

This conversation seemed so…normal…compared to what they'd been through together so far. It was a nice reprieve. No matter how temporary.

"I like simple breakfasts mostly. A couple pieces of toast, maybe some eggs and I'm good to go."

"Are you feeling okay this morning? I wasn't sure after your allergy attack, how long you'd feel the aftereffects." Andrew grabbed a mug and poured her some coffee, adding that he'd sanitized the coffeepot just to be safe.

Natalie shrugged. "I'm about as well as can be expected. You?"

"The same. Every little noise woke me up last night. Rambo snored too." He glanced at his dog, who faithfully sat watching him cook, no doubt hoping his human might drop something. "I'm praying that today might provide some answers."

"I agree. Because I don't know how much longer I can live like this. Then again, who am I to say that? Especially considering what my sister might be going through right now." Another frown tugged at her lips.

"Everything you're feeling is normal," he assured her.

His words caught her by surprise—mostly because he sounded so understanding and calming. She deeply appreciated those two qualities. In fact, she craved them right now.

"Is this what they call survivor's guilt?" she asked.

"I don't know all the mental health terms people are using these days," Andrew said. "I just know that what you've been dealing with is highly emotional. I think you're handling it really well."

"All things considered?" Natalie tilted her head and grinned.

"Exactly."

"You've worked with people and situations similar to mine before?" She took a sip of her coffee. It tasted good. Really good.

The caffeine energy boost was a nice bonus.

He shrugged and turned a piece of bacon. "I've worked

abductions and threats and just about anything else you can think of."

Natalie turned her attention from her problems a moment. She wanted to know more about Andrew, but she sensed there was still a lot about himself that he was keeping at bay.

She leaned back in her barstool and observed him a moment.

He was no doubt handsome. But it was his integrity and character that had truly caught her attention. She'd never met anyone like him before.

He'd gone out of his way to help her, expecting nothing in return. It wasn't something she often came across these days.

These circumstances had pulled them close in such a short time period. But she felt as if he were someone she'd known forever—and that she always wanted to have in her life.

What did these thoughts even mean?

She wasn't exactly sure—nor was she sure he felt the same way. She thought he did. She thought she'd seen a spark of attraction in his gaze.

But this wasn't exactly the best time to strike up a romance—not that she was looking for love. Natalie had a feeling he wasn't either.

She cleared her throat as she turned her mind from those thoughts. "Did you ever work with any country music stars out in Nashville?"

He finished cooking the bacon and added pancake batter to the griddle as he answered. "We actually do work quite a bit with people in the music industry. Stalkers, threats, overzealous fans. You name it."

Natalie felt better knowing he was experienced. It was good to have someone to rely on. It had been a long time since she'd thought she needed anybody.

But she knew that wasn't true. *Everyone* needed people in their lives, during both the good times and the bad.

A few minutes later, Andrew placed a plate in front of her, complete with pancakes and bacon. Then he set some syrup beside the plate and refilled her coffee.

"Thank you." A surge of gratitude rushed through her. She wasn't used to having people look out for her.

The feeling was nice. She could get used to this.

Andrew grabbed his own plate and then sat beside her at the breakfast bar. They lifted a prayer before eating.

She stared out the window at the mountains and let out a deep breath. "I never considered myself a mountain girl before. But I wish I was here in different circumstances. There's something calming about the tranquility out here."

"I agree," Andrew said. "I've always loved it here. The city is nice, but the older I get the more I appreciate peace and quiet."

She imagined for a minute what it might be like to live out here. To move away from the city.

It wasn't something she'd ever considered before. But what would a change like that be like in her life? Her life back in Cincinnati had been so hectic and busy. She thought she'd liked that.

But, in truth, being busy helped her to forget about her problems. To forget about her father's death. Her strained relationship with her sister. How she had no one she could truly rely on.

Natalie had only taken a few bites of her breakfast when her phone buzzed.

She grabbed it from her pocket and looked at the screen. Someone had texted her.

When she clicked on the message, she gasped, and her appetite—and peace—completely disappeared.

It was a picture of her sister.

Lexi was in a dark room. Tied to a chair with a gag around her mouth.

The look in her eyes was pure desperation.

"We have to call the police." Andrew stared at the picture of Lexi, his jaw hardening. "This is the solid proof we need that something did happen to her. Detective Caruso won't be able to deny this anymore."

Natalie nodded, that glazed look filling her eyes again. "Okay. Can you make the call?"

"Absolutely. They'll probably want to come out here and talk to us. Are you okay with that?"

"Yes. Whatever I need to do to help my sister."

Andrew grabbed his phone and stepped away to make the call. Detective Caruso answered and said he'd be there within twenty minutes.

No sooner had Andrew ended the call did his phone ring again.

It was his friend Grayson from Cincinnati.

Andrew quickly answered, hoping Grayson was calling with an update.

"I just heard something this morning I thought you'd want to know," Grayson started. "The ex-boyfriend I told you about? Our suspect with the German shepherd who disappeared?"

"What about him?" Andrew's muscles tensed as he waited for his reply.

"I got word this morning he's been located."

Andrew's heart raced faster. "What? Where is he?"

"Canada. I suppose that's good news that we found him. But whatever is happening to you wherever you are...well, it wasn't Daniel. He's been there for a while now."

His thoughts continued to race. "Did he confess to the murders?"

"No, he said he had nothing to do with them. Claimed

he didn't even know what happened. That he'd gone to Canada because he'd wanted to go off-grid and reconsider his future after his breakup."

"You believed him?"

"I wasn't there to question him myself. But the authorities I talked to seem to think his story is true. But they're still trying to put together all the evidence, just to be sure."

Andrew felt his jaw tightening. That wasn't necessarily the news he'd been wanting.

If not Daniel, then who?

The madman taunting Natalie was still faceless and nameless. "Thanks. I appreciate you looking into that for me."

"No problem. I hope you find the answers you're looking for."

Andrew ended the call and shoved his phone back into his pocket. He saw Natalie staring at him from the breakfast bar and strode toward her to give her the update.

Her shoulders slumped at the news. She had to be feeling as if she just couldn't catch a break. Anyone in her shoes would.

"At least we know we can rule out this guy as a suspect," Andrew told her. "I hope you don't mind that I made the call to my friend. I didn't tell him where you're staying right now because I didn't think you wanted anyone to know."

"I don't mind at all. I appreciate you being discreet as well. But I'm still just so shaken up by all this." Natalie rubbed her arms. "I just have no idea who could be behind this. The police were so focused on Daniel… I feel like I'm starting out from square one."

"Maybe it was someone else who was upset with Drexel. Or there was that man you ran into here—Nathan, right? And he mentioned a coworker, Gary, who's been bad-mouthing you. It could be any of those people."

She frowned. She hated to think that anyone she knew might be behind this.

As tires rumbled outside, Rambo sat up, his ears perking.

Andrew's shoulders tensed as he made his way to the window.

He glanced outside and saw the police had arrived. "Caruso is here."

Thanks to that picture, they now had proof that something had happened to Lexi.

Hopefully, with the help of the local cops, they could find the missing woman before another tragic event scarred Natalie's life.

SEVENTEEN

Natalie bristled when Detective Caruso stepped inside.

She didn't like this guy *or* trust him.

Could he be involved with Lexi's disappearance somehow?

She didn't see how—she doubted he was connected with what happened in Cincinnati. But she still didn't like him.

"I got this photograph in a text this morning." Natalie handed the detective her phone as they all stood in Andrew's living room. Caruso had brought another detective with him—a man with salt-and-pepper hair who appeared to be in his fifties.

Caruso looked at the photo of Lexi and grimaced. "I don't like the way this looks. You have no idea who sent this?"

Natalie shook her head. "I have no idea. Should I reply?"

"Not a good idea. Not yet, at least." He shifted, his gaze flickering back and forth from Natalie to Andrew. "Has anything else happened since you came into the station yesterday?"

Natalie gave him a rundown of yesterday's events, and Caruso made grunting sounds as he jotted notes on his notepad. They'd already told him some of what had happened, but she hadn't reported everything.

Now she had no choice. She even told him about what happened back in Cincinnati in detail.

With her sister's life on the line, Natalie had to do whatever she could to find her—even expose her own secrets to this cop.

When she finished, Caruso asked, "Is there anything else you can think of?"

"There was one other thing." Natalie wasn't sure if she should bring this up or not, but she couldn't seem to stop herself. She needed to get everything out there. "I heard that you and my sister used to date."

Caruso's cheeks reddened as if he hadn't expected her to know that. "We went on a couple of casual dates. Not enough to say we were *dating*."

"Then she told you that she didn't like you anymore," Natalie continued. "Is that one of the reasons why you didn't want to pursue this case yesterday?"

His eyes narrowed with offense. "Of course not. I'm a professional. I take my job responsibilities seriously."

Natalie stared at him, making no secret of the fact she didn't believe him.

"I meant what I said when I told you we need forty-eight hours unless other things arise." Caruso pointed to her phone. "This is definitely something that has gotten our attention."

"I just want to make sure that your personal feelings aren't clouding your judgment right now." She needed to make it clear to him that this wasn't a game. Her sister's life was on the line and whatever grudge he might hold against her wasn't appropriate right now.

His scowl deepened. "I can assure you that my personal feelings won't dictate my actions. Now, if it's okay with you, I'd like to go search her place to see if there's any evidence that has been left behind."

"Of course." Natalie rubbed her arms as she wondered what he might find there. "I'll give you the key."

Caruso's lips flicked down in a frown. "You can come with me if you'd like—"

Natalie was shaking her head before he could finish his sentence. "I've already looked for anything I could find. I didn't find anything. I'm not even sure what I'm supposed to be looking for."

"That's why I'm going to check it out. I'm trained for these things. I'll keep you updated. If you hear anything else, then please let us know."

"Will do."

Natalie stared at the detectives as they left.

She still didn't like Caruso and couldn't help but think that he was hiding something. The other detective didn't say much of anything and had let Caruso take the lead.

She could picture these two playing good cop, bad cop like they do on TV. Natalie didn't care which detective took on which role. She just wanted her sister to be found safe and as soon as possible.

At least Caruso seemed to be taking her seriously now.

But that didn't mean she trusted him in the slightest.

Maybe he wasn't connected to what had happened in Cincinnati.

But that didn't mean he wasn't somehow involved in all of this.

And if he was, she just had to figure out how.

Neither Andrew nor Natalie seemed to have much of an appetite for their breakfast after their visit with Detective Caruso. Not to mention their pancakes and bacon were now cold.

Andrew fed his leftover bacon to Rambo, who seemed grateful for the turn of luck. Their loss was the dog's gain.

As Andrew cleaned the kitchen, he watched Natalie pace in front of the fireplace.

The police were over at Lexi's place right now checking it out. He wondered if they'd find something he hadn't. He hadn't exactly done an exhaustive search of the place. And the guy who'd abducted Lexi may have even gone back to wreak more havoc.

Either way, Andrew didn't like where this was going.

He didn't want to stay in the cabin all day—and he knew that Natalie didn't either.

But there was nowhere left for them to search. They'd run out of leads. That man had sent them that picture as a means of shaking them up—and it had worked. But the sender hadn't offered any other further instructions.

He'd played with the idea of texting the man back also. But he agreed with Caruso—it was better not to engage and to wait for this guy's next move.

Andrew walked to the window and moved the curtain aside. He wanted to know when the detectives finished investigating next door. For now, it looked like they were all still there.

Several minutes later, he saw police cars go by on the road in the distance.

They'd left Lexi's house already and, since there was no phone call, he could only assume they hadn't found anything.

"They're headed out already." Andrew shook his head. "I thought they'd be there a lot longer."

"Maybe they're following a lead of some sort?" Natalie suggested. "Maybe they're planning to go back a little later. Either way, I hope Caruso remembers to bring my key back." Natalie joined him at the window.

"If not, we'll give him a call later and remind him." Andrew wasn't sure if Caruso would think to return it or not. "He might still need to hold on to it for a bit."

Natalie paused as she followed his gaze. "I feel like I'm losing my mind."

"I know. The waiting can sometimes be the hardest part." Before he could say anything else, his phone buzzed.

The area code indicated it was someone from Nashville.

His heart rate quickened. Was someone calling about his job? Was this the moment he learned whether or not he was permanently suspended or if his old position would be restored?

He was expecting to hear something any day now.

He'd told himself he was okay with stepping away from police work. That he'd find something else equally as fulfilling. But the events of the last two days had reignited that passion inside him. The passion to remain on the force. To be a part of the team that makes a dent in the various crimes affecting the area.

He loved his job. He wanted to keep serving and protecting people as a detective.

He hadn't realized how much until the possibility of not being able to do it became a very real, tangible option.

Andrew almost didn't want to answer. But he had to.

He glanced at Natalie, who stared at him with curiosity. "Excuse me for a moment."

Then Andrew slipped into his bedroom to take the phone call, praying for the best.

What was that about?

Natalie had seen Andrew's face go pale when he looked at his phone screen.

Was there something he wasn't telling her? Did this phone call pertain to her sister or was it something else unrelated?

Natalie wasn't sure.

She wanted to believe she could trust Andrew. And her gut told her she could.

But she hoped her gut instincts were right.

The emotional trauma of recent events had left her with brain fog and had her questioning herself—which was new for her. Before this all started happening, she'd been so self-assured. So confident.

But not anymore. She'd learned a certain humbleness throughout this entire experience.

She might not be able to determine the outcome of the situation, especially the things that were totally out of her control, but she could most definitely make the most of it and learn something.

A few minutes later, Andrew stepped back in the room and shoved his phone back into his pocket. "Sorry. It was someone from Nashville calling about work."

"Is everything okay?"

"It's fine," he quickly insisted, not offering any more information.

What exactly had led Andrew here? He'd never opened up about it, and Natalie hadn't felt right asking him. But she saw something deep and painful swirling in the depths of his eyes.

For all she knew, he could have a woman waiting for him back in Nashville.

The thought left her feeling unsettled, to say the least.

She'd grown fond of him, more than she'd counted on.

Natalie wanted to know more. She wanted to know about his past. Wanted to know if there were ways she might help.

As they stood in the living room another moment, Rambo let out a growl as he stared at the door. The next moment, he darted toward the window and his paws went to the sill.

He nuzzled the curtain out of the way as he stared at something, slobber flying from his jowls as his barking turned ferocious.

"Andrew…" Her heart rate sped at the sight of the anger in the dog. "He's scaring me."

Natalie pushed away the flashbacks that wanted to hit her.

"He's not going to hurt you." Andrew raced toward the window and peered out. "He senses something, or someone, outside."

"Is the guy back again?" she murmured.

"I'm not sure. But there's only one way to find out."

Fear gripped her. "You're going to go out there again?"

"I have to know. I'm tired of these games, and I'm sure you are too." His gaze locked with hers. "Stay here. Keep Rambo with you. I'll be right back."

She nodded. She didn't have much choice in the matter. Not if there was someone lurking around outside.

And the dog was insistent that he'd seen something.

But for now, Natalie would wait…and pray for Andrew to return in one piece.

EIGHTEEN

Natalie wanted to look out the window, but she didn't let herself.

She was afraid to get too close in case someone started shooting again.

But Andrew still wasn't back yet. It had probably only been a few minutes, but it felt like hours.

Was he okay?

She hadn't heard any other sounds, so she could only assume he was.

But the last thing Natalie wanted was for someone else to get hurt because of some psycho who was targeting her.

Was this about her? She'd assumed the murder had been about those Drexel executives. It was the only thing that made sense at the time. That she'd walked in on the crime scene just as the killer was finishing up.

But maybe there was more to it.

What if he'd realized not everyone was there? What if he'd been waiting for her?

The thought struck more terror into her.

Natalie wasn't sure what to think. So much had happened in a short amount of time. It seemed as if this killer was relentless.

She checked the time on her phone. Andrew had been gone ten minutes now.

What if something was wrong?

Rambo whined at the window as if he wanted to go outside and check also.

She called the dog over to her and waited, hardly able to contain herself. Absently, she reached down and rubbed Rambo's head.

The dog brought her such a strange comfort.

He was nothing like the dog that had attacked her. The dog that had been bred and trained for violence.

Not Rambo. He'd been trained for service.

People could be a lot like that, couldn't they? Even her and Lexi.

When their parents had divorced when Natalie was thirteen, Lexi had gone to live with their mom while Natalie stayed with their more stable dad.

That had been a transformative moment for both of them. Their different choices had shaped their futures and caused them to head in opposite directions.

Natalie cherished the time she'd had with her dad. And seeing how Lexi turned out, Natalie knew she'd made the right decision by choosing not to live with her mom.

A child needed stability. Someone to look up to. Someone they felt safe with.

Natalie wasn't sure her mom had provided any of those things for Lexi.

If she'd only known… Dad would have done something about it. Or at least he would've tried.

Natalie shoved aside those thoughts for now and waited.

She'd promised Andrew she would stay inside, but the waiting was killing her.

Natalie hadn't heard any gunshots, and she decided it was time to at least glance outside. To see if she could spot anything going on. As she rose to her feet, her phone buzzed.

Her heart rate quickened.

Was it Andrew? Was he texting to say he was okay?

But it was the same number as before—the same number that had sent that picture of Lexi.

Her heart beat harder.

Not now. She didn't want any more bad news.

Natalie's hands trembled so much as she held her phone that she feared she would drop the device.

But she finally managed to click on the message.

I have my gun trained on your boyfriend. If you don't want him to die, step out the back door. Walk down the mountain and keep walking. Leave right now or he'll die.

Natalie's thoughts swirled.

She knew she shouldn't leave.

The man behind this could be bluffing.

But with Andrew still gone how could she be certain of anything?

How could she turn her back on the situation? What if this guy was serious? If Andrew's life was in Natalie's hands?

She paced to the window and looked out front, hoping to see Andrew. Hoping she might give him that update.

But he was nowhere to be seen.

She could text him, but would the killer see Andrew check his phone? Would he know she was trying to communicate with him?

It was just too risky. She was on her own.

Natalie looked down at Rambo and frowned. "I don't have any choice but to do this, big guy. Stay here and guard the place, okay?"

He whined, almost as if warning her it was a bad idea.

She knew it was.

But how would she be able to live with herself knowing she could have done something to save Andrew but didn't?

She knew the answer to that question.

With one more glance at Rambo, she grabbed a flashlight and her jacket and stepped toward the back door. Her entire body quivered with fear and adrenaline.

She hoped she wouldn't regret this.

But she had a feeling she would.

Andrew heard Rambo barking inside the house. Then the sound became more frantic.

Alarm raced through him.

Had something happened to Natalie?

He'd been wandering these woods for at least ten minutes, and he still hadn't found anything. Whatever had alerted Rambo that something was out here, appeared to be long gone.

It could have been an animal.

Or maybe it had just been a distraction. What if someone had lured him outside to get him away from Natalie?

His muscles tightened.

Andrew wouldn't put anything past this guy at this point.

He hurried back to the house, a new sense of urgency washing through him.

But just as he reached the front porch, his foot hit something.

A wire.

As it did, something whooshed through the air and sliced into his biceps. He let out a grunt as the pain hit him.

The object had cut through his shirtsleeve, and blood came down his arm.

He looked over and saw an arrow had skimmed his flesh and embedded into a nearby tree.

The realization stunned him.

Someone had set up a trap outside his house while he'd been out searching the woods.

Whoever this was either had professional training or had thought long and hard about ways to take people out.

Even more urgency raced through him.

The man had been within feet of Natalie, and he hadn't even known it.

Andrew rushed into the cabin.

Rambo greeted him at the door, his bark insistent.

"What is it, boy?" Andrew leaned closer, ignoring the pain in his arm.

He scanned the room. Then he checked the other rooms.

Natalie was gone.

His heart pounded harder.

Had someone taken her?

All his doors had been secure. Someone would only have gotten in if Natalie had let them in. Andrew didn't think she'd do that—not unless she had a really good reason.

His gaze stopped on the coffee table.

Natalie's phone was there.

He walked to it and tapped the screen. The most recent text message showed on the lock screen.

As Andrew read the words, his blood went cold.

Of course, Natalie wouldn't have been able to say no to this request—not if it removed the target from his back and meant her sister might be returned safely.

He wished he'd had a chance to tell her not to endanger herself on his account.

He could take care of himself.

As more blood seeped down his arm and dripped onto the floor, his worry for Natalie grew.

Natalie leaving the safety of the cabin was a bad idea.

This man was extremely dangerous.

Exactly what did this man have in store for her?

The killer wasn't planning to let either Natalie or Lexi live through this. Andrew was certain of it.

He grabbed an old T-shirt and wrapped it around his wound to help staunch the bleeding, then grabbed the leash and attached it to Rambo's collar. "We've got to find her, boy."

Rambo barked in agreement.

The message had only been sent seven minutes ago. Natalie shouldn't be too far away at this point.

Andrew double-checked that his gun was in his holster as he stepped out the back door.

Normally, he'd have to give Rambo something to track her scent. But the dog seemed to know exactly what—and who—he was looking for.

Rambo began to pull him down the side of the mountain at a fast pace. Andrew had to slow the canine so they could watch their steps on the steep decline.

As he walked, he scanned everything around him, but he hadn't seen Natalie yet.

Too many things obstructed his view from here—mostly rocky outcroppings and trees.

He wanted to call for her, but he didn't dare.

Instead, Rambo towed him along, leading him toward Natalie…he hoped.

As Natalie stepped around a tree, someone reached from around it and grabbed her. A hand covered her mouth before she could scream.

She hadn't even seen the man's face.

But she knew it was him. The man behind this mayhem and those murders.

"Good girl," he whispered in her ear. "Now it's time for the final payback."

Final payback? What did that mean?

It almost sounded like all of this had been for revenge or something. But did that even make sense? What had Natalie ever done for him to want revenge?

"Now, I'm going to release my hand from your mouth. If you scream, I'll kill you right here. Right now. Got it?"

Natalie nodded.

As soon as he did, she demanded, "Where's my sister?"

"Your sister? Why would you ask me that?"

"Because you took her. I know you did."

He let out a chuckle. "Is that what you think? You must have an overactive imagination."

Why was he playing games with her?

"Is she okay? You better not have hurt her."

"Now you're threatening me? You've got some nerve, don't you?"

Before she could say anything else, the man's hand covered her mouth again.

"It's been fun. But I'm running out of patience."

She hadn't screamed. Was he going to kill her right here and now anyway?

But if this man killed Natalie, then what would happen to Lexi? Would he just kill her also?

She shouldn't have come out here. She should have waited. Thought it through.

But the man hadn't allowed her time for that. He'd planned this too carefully.

Natalie heard a stick crack in the distance.

The man bristled behind her.

Then he leaned forward, almost as if peering around the tree.

As he did, Natalie caught a glimpse of Rambo and Andrew.

They were at least thirty feet away.

But they were there.

Her breath caught—first with hope that she'd be rescued, then with fear that something would happen to them. In this short amount of time, she'd grown to care about both of them. She didn't want to see them hurt.

It was bad enough she'd gotten them involved in this in the first place.

This man could ambush Andrew. Step out and shoot him.

She couldn't let that happen.

She had to warn him. But how?

Then she saw it.

Grabbing a dead branch on the tree beside her, Natalie yanked down on it. The dry wood snapped in two, cracking loudly.

The sound of Andrew's footsteps suddenly stopped.

"Natalie?" he called.

"You think you're so smart, don't you?" the man whispered in her ear. "I don't care how many people I have to kill first, as long as you die too."

A shudder coursed through her.

He really was going to try and kill Andrew, wasn't he?

"Stop right there," the man shouted to Andrew. "Don't make a move."

He dragged her away from the tree and into Andrew's line of sight.

Andrew held up his hands as his eyes widened. "Don't hurt her. Let her go."

"You weren't supposed to live long enough to follow her."

"Your little arrow missed its mark. You're not going to get away with this," Andrew called.

Arrow? What arrow?

"I've gotten away with it so far. This is just the final puzzle piece I need to put in place. People like Natalie need to pay."

Natalie's thoughts continued to race.

What had she ever done to make someone this angry with her? She had no idea.

The man tensed again, anger seeming to thread through his taut muscles. "I mean it. Don't come any closer."

He pulled her back a step and, as he did, Natalie looked down and sucked in a breath.

She teetered near the edge of a cliff. She'd estimate it was probably twelve feet to the bottom.

But twelve feet could do a lot of damage.

"If you come any closer, I'll kill her," he warned.

Natalie glanced back at Andrew.

"I won't." He remained in place. "Just don't hurt her."

"You should have never come after me. This has nothing to do with you. I only set that trap so you wouldn't be able to mess this up."

Trap? What had happened? Did it have something to do with an arrow?

Her heart pounded harder. She didn't like the sound of that.

"You just need to leave Natalie alone," Andrew said. "Let Lexi go. Let's end this."

Natalie heard the diplomacy in his voice. She appreciated his effort to negotiate.

But she didn't think the tactic would work on this guy. He'd been determined to end her for two months now.

"It's too late. You being here isn't part of my plan," the man muttered with a grunt, almost as if something had flipped inside him. "I really wanted to take my time with this. You've ruined everything!"

The next instant, the man pushed Natalie into the open air beside her, and she felt herself falling.

NINETEEN

Andrew saw Natalie disappear off the cliff.

Heard her scream, but it was cut short almost immediately. Almost as if...

No. He couldn't think like that. He knew this area. There weren't any deep ravines up this way. Just some smaller outcroppings.

She would be okay. She had to be. But she would need his help.

Andrew and Rambo sprinted toward Natalie as the man darted in the opposite direction.

But when Andrew paused at the cliff's edge, he saw her body lying there.

She wasn't moving.

His heart beat even harder.

No...

He glanced at the man again as he vanished into the woods.

Andrew had to make a choice.

Save Natalie or go after this guy.

It was a no-brainer.

He and Rambo scrambled down the rocks to get to Natalie.

Just as they reached her side, she moaned.

Andrew's heart leapt into his throat. She was still alive.

Thank You, Lord!

But he wasn't sure what kind of shape she was in.

He knelt beside her. Her eyes were closed.

"I'm here, Natalie."

She said nothing.

Quickly, he checked her pulse.

Her heart still felt strong.

Then Andrew felt along her legs and arms, searching for any breaks.

He didn't feel anything out of place.

He leaned over her. "Natalie, can you hear me?"

Another soft moan escaped.

"I'm going to get you help, okay? Just stay with me."

Finally, Natalie's eyes slowly opened, and she blinked. She let out another moan before murmuring, "Andrew…"

He squeezed her hand. "It's okay. I'm here."

"The man…" She pointed in the direction where the guy had been.

"It's too late. He's gone now."

"But…" She squinted as she tried to sit up.

Andrew gently pushed her back down. "Don't move yet. I need to make sure your spine is okay. Where does it hurt?"

Natalie squeezed her eyes shut again and groaned. "I don't know. Everywhere."

Andrew pulled out his phone to call for help. But when he glanced at it, his fears were confirmed. There was no signal out here.

His heart raced even faster.

He couldn't leave Natalie here to go get help. But that meant he'd need to come up with a plan to get her back to his cabin. Would she be able to walk? Or would he need to carry her?

That's what he needed to figure out.

"I know this is hard," he told her. "But I need to see if you broke anything. Okay?"

Natalie nodded and groaned again.

A small trickle of blood came from her forehead, but that cut could easily be bandaged.

Andrew checked her arms and legs one more time before feeling her ribs.

Thankfully, everything appeared to be unbroken.

"I'm going to help you sit up," he murmured as he peered at her. "Are you okay with that?"

Natalie nodded.

Leaning behind her, Andrew slowly pushed her into a sitting position.

She didn't let out any sudden yelps of pain.

If she'd managed to fall off a cliff without breaking anything, then she was a very fortunate woman.

Andrew had seen falls like that take people out before.

"How does your head feel? Did it take a direct hit?"

"I'm a little off balance, but no, I didn't hit my head. I tried to tuck and roll the best I could. It's my knees that are killing me."

Hurt knees were better than a cracked skull.

He lifted another prayer of thanks, along with a request that everything would continue to pan out for them and not take a turn for the worse.

"I got a text…" she started, her voice cracking.

"I know. I saw it."

"I didn't know what to do. I didn't want to believe he had his sights on you, but I couldn't take that risk—"

"Shh," Andrew said. "It's okay. He probably planned it that way. He knew if you had too much time to think about it then you would have stayed where you were."

"Are you okay?" Suddenly, Natalie's own pain seemed to be forgotten as she looked up at him.

"I'm fine. I'm just worried about you right now."

She frowned as she stared at his biceps. "You're not fine. You're bleeding."

"It's just a flesh wound. Come on. We need to get somewhere safe."

"I just want to get back to the cabin. I want to find my sister."

"Okay. Then let's see if we can get you to your feet. We'll get back inside and make a plan from there."

After some struggling, Natalie managed to stand.

She could put weight on both of her legs, which was all he needed to know.

Then Andrew began to help her back up the mountainside.

This all seemed like a nightmare, Natalie mused.

If Andrew hadn't shown up when he did, what would that man have done to her? Would he have taken her to Lexi? Or would he have killed her in the woods?

So many things he'd said to her didn't make any sense.

Now it's time for the final payback.

Your sister? Is that what you think? You must have an overactive imagination.

Payback... That one still tripped her up.

Payback for what? It didn't make sense.

Did this guy think she'd wronged him? How?

Finally, after a brutal uphill walk, she and Andrew reached his cabin.

Andrew ushered her inside and had her sit on the couch. Then he grabbed a first aid kit and began to doctor the cut on her forehead. She also had scrapes on her elbows and hands, her knees were bruised and swollen, and her hip was sore.

But things could have been much worse. She knew that for certain.

Natalie tried not to wince as the ointment touched her

wound. "Which direction did this guy run? I thought it was nothing but miles of wilderness back there."

Andrew dabbed her face again with a gauze pad. "It mostly is. But there *is* a trail that runs back there maybe a half a mile back."

"Where does it lead?"

"It's a big loop, but it starts and ends…" He paused. "Wait a minute. Part of the trail is actually a service road the park rangers use. A service road that ends at the parking lot that Rambo led us to when we were looking for Lexi."

"That's how he's coming and going. Just like we thought when Rambo led us to the parking area."

"So that means he's probably heading back that way to pick up his vehicle."

She shook her head. "I just can't believe any of this."

"I know." He dabbed her wound once more before leaning back.

"Should we call the police and tell them what's happening?"

"Absolutely. Especially since we think we know where he's headed. Even if they don't catch him in the parking lot, they can check the service road as he tries to get away."

Andrew pulled out his phone to make the call.

But before he could, tires sounded on gravel outside.

Natalie froze. "Or maybe he cut to the chase and came right back here to finish us off?"

Andrew stood and glanced out the window. "It's not him. It's the police. They're back."

Natalie remained tense. "I don't know if that's good news or bad news."

"Me either." Andrew opened the door.

Detective Caruso stood there.

Natalie knew as soon as she saw his expression that he didn't have good news.

She pressed her eyes shut.

Please don't let him tell me that he found Lexi. That she's dead.

But she sensed bad news was coming whether she was ready to hear it or not.

"What happened to you?" Caruso examined her, not bothering to hide his surprise at her condition.

"We were just about to call you." Andrew visibly bristled. "The man who took Lexi…he was here. He grabbed Natalie and then pushed her off a cliff. We just got back to the house."

"What happened to the guy?"

"He took off."

Caruso's gaze narrowed. "You should've let us know right away."

"We literally just got back to the house, and I was about to call you. We had no service out there behind the house. You know how spotty it can be in this area sometimes."

The detective frowned. "I'll have my guys scour the woods, just in case. But I suspect this guy is long gone."

Andrew told Caruso his theory about the service road, and Caruso sent some patrol officers that way to look for anyone leaving the area.

Andrew shifted and put his hands on his hips. "So what originally brought you back here?"

The man's jaw hardened. "We searched Lexi's cabin, but we didn't find anything of particular note. Then we went to the restaurant and talked to a couple people there. That eventually led us to go to Dylan Murphy's house to talk to him."

"And?" Natalie stared at him hopefully.

"When we went inside, we found Dylan."

"What do you mean you found him?" Natalie thought she knew the truth, but she wasn't ready to accept it.

"Someone shot him point-blank. He's…dead."

TWENTY

Andrew certainly hadn't heard correctly. "Dylan is dead?"

Something gleamed in Caruso's gaze. Accusation maybe.

"That's right," he muttered. "When was the last time that you two saw him?"

Andrew and Natalie exchanged a look.

"He was here last night," Andrew said.

Caruso squinted. "Here? At the cabin?"

"Yes. He came by here and said he was looking for Lexi. But we told him she wasn't here."

"How did that conversation end? Did you have an altercation?"

"No, we ended it on good terms," Natalie said. "We all just wanted the best for Lexi. We wanted to find her. He told us if he thought of somewhere she might be he'd let us know and then he left."

"Where were you last night?" The detective examined Andrew with a good dose of suspicion in his gaze.

"Where was I? I was right here with Natalie." Andrew shifted as his eyes narrowed. "I just told you Dylan came by, and we talked. What are you getting at? Am I a suspect?"

"You two were likely the last ones to see him alive. I

heard you had a terse conversation with him in the parking lot of Alpine Bistro." He shrugged. "I'm just trying to cover all my bases."

"I'm sure you are." Andrew narrowed his eyes. "We were just talking. There was nothing terse about our conversation."

"I just wanted you to be aware that something's going on," Caruso said coolly. "I don't like whatever it is that's happening here."

"Neither do we," Natalie said.

Caruso examined her a moment. "Is that your car out there? The one that probably cost 90K?"

She bristled. "It is."

"You have a cushy advertising job back in the city, don't you? I looked you up."

"I quit, if you must know. I'm not sure how this pertains to anything."

"I'm just saying…you two seem to be right in the middle of all this. It all seemed to start happening when you showed up, Natalie." Caruso's gaze skittered back to Andrew. "I want to believe that I can trust you and what you're telling me."

"You can." Andrew raised his chin. "Why are you even bringing this up?"

"Because I don't trust any police officer who takes bribes."

Andrew reeled.

So word had gotten back to Caruso about the fiasco in Nashville.

And now Caruso was trying to get under his skin for some reason.

It wouldn't work.

Andrew didn't owe this man any type of explanation.

Instead, he just gave him a death glare and waited for him to leave.

* * *

What did that mean? Natalie wondered once Caruso left.

Taking bribes? It certainly didn't sound like something Andrew would do.

But how could she say that? She hardly even knew the man.

So why did she feel so certain that he'd never do something like that?

Natalie supposed it was the character he exuded.

They looked at each other for a moment before finally Andrew sat down beside her.

"What was Caruso talking about?" Natalie shifted to face him.

"The truth is that the leave of absence from my job I told you about? It was because I was suspended from my position back in Nashville pending an investigation."

"What are they investigating?"

"Let me back up a little bit. It all started when I caught my fiancée cheating on me with another officer. I confronted her about it. But her dad was the chief, and he took her side of things. Things got tricky for me at work after that. Especially after I broke things off with her. After that, she seemed to have a vendetta against me. She wanted to get rid of me altogether. Said it was too traumatic to see me around the station when she went to visit her father at work."

"That's terrible. But…what did she do to get you suspended?"

"She planted some drugs from a bust we did in my locker—on a day where there just so happened to be a random search. Then she made up lies to go along with it, said she'd suspected me of taking bribes and that's why *she'd* broken up with *me*."

"And everyone believed her?"

"It didn't matter if everyone believed her. Her dad believed her. A formal investigation into me was launched."

"I'm so sorry. I can't even imagine what that must have been like."

"It was tough, to say the least. That was actually Sarah who called me earlier."

Natalie's eyes widened. "Why did she call you? You said it was about work?"

"It was about work. She started out saying she wanted to apologize to me in person, that what she did was wrong. My gut feeling is that she and this guy she was seeing ended things, and Sarah realized she'd make a big mistake. She said she could make the charges against me disappear. I could have my job back. All she had to do was talk to her dad."

"And what did she want you to do? Take her back? Pretend all that she did never happened?"

"Pretty much."

"So if you take her back, she makes the charges—that she made up against you in the first place—disappear?"

"That's right."

"And if you don't?"

"She stays silent. I face the false charges. My word against hers."

Natalie shook her head. "I can't believe your fiancée would do that to you."

He nodded and rubbed his neck. "Unfortunately, she did. She wasn't willing to look like the bad guy in the situation so instead, she ran my name through the mud."

"That's horrible. I'm sorry." Natalie rested her hand on his arm. "Did she actually expect you to forgive her and take her back?"

"I have forgiven her since then. But that doesn't mean I'm willing to reconcile. I tried to explain that to her, but she didn't want to hear it. She thought forgiveness meant that I was willing to jump right back in and pick up where we'd left off. She didn't understand that forgiving her actually helped me be free of her."

"You were blessed to get out of that relationship. I know it was painful but…can you imagine if you'd gone through with it and married her?"

"No, I can't. I figure that everything happens for a reason and that I'll learn and grow through this experience also. I just really need my name to be cleared."

"Wait. Did I misunderstand? You're not going to get back with her, are you?"

"Not a chance. I'll figure out another way to fix this."

"That's good to hear." Natalie swallowed hard. "If it makes you feel better, I've come through a terrible relationship. I was dating someone before the dog attack. Things didn't end well for me either."

He shifted as he studied her. "What happened?"

"I think he feared I would be permanently disfigured or that he'd have to take care of me. That wasn't in his plans for his future. He had too much life left to live to be tied down with someone who may not be fully functional— his words, not mine."

Andrew squeezed her hand.

She didn't pull away.

"Do you know when he chose to have this conversation with me? When he came to visit me in the hospital. First thing he did was ask me how many stitches I had. Then he looked at the size of my bandages. Next thing I knew, we were through."

"That's horrible," he murmured. "I'm really sorry. A guy like that doesn't deserve you."

Their gazes caught.

They'd both been through terrible circumstances.

And here they were in a terrible circumstance again.

When it came to moments like this, a person could do one of two things.

They could whine and complain about it. Or they could let it make them stronger.

Natalie knew which one that she was going to choose.

"I also believe everything happens for a reason," Natalie said as her gaze drifted to Andrew's lips. She'd been attracted to him from the start. The more she got to know him the stronger her attraction to him became.

Andrew cupped her cheek with his hand as he leaned closer. "You're an amazing woman, Natalie Pearson. I'm so glad we ran into each other in the woods that night."

"You…feel it too? A connection between us?"

"I do. Natalie, I never expected to feel this…"

"I know what you mean." She nibbled on her bottom lip as she stared into his eyes. "I'd sworn off men. Until I ran into you."

"You literally ran into me. And you bounced off, if I recall correctly."

"I did, but then you caught me."

"I did, didn't I?" The next instant, he leaned closer.

His fingers tangled with her hair. She felt the body heat rippling from him.

Natalie never thought that while in the midst of life-or-death circumstances she might find romance. She was a planner by nature. Practical.

But Andrew had swooped into her life and impressed her like no other man had.

Natalie closed her eyes as she anticipated his kiss.

But before their lips met, his phone rang, jarring them from the moment.

TWENTY-ONE

Andrew's thoughts shifted from the near kiss to what Caruso had to say.

He'd said police had found a vehicle in the parking lot, so they could only assume the man was still in the woods somewhere.

He had also told Andrew they'd searched the woods and hadn't found the bad guy. They were pulling out and calling off the search.

Caruso might have given up, but that didn't mean Andrew had to.

Another plan formed in his mind.

He couldn't believe he was about to suggest what he was.

But he knew he'd regret it if he kept this idea to himself.

"There's one thing we might be able to do." He shifted toward Natalie on the couch.

Natalie sat up straighter. "What's that?"

"That guy was right outside the house. Rambo could probably follow his scent. I'm not sure where it would lead us, but it couldn't hurt to find out."

"Let's do it," Natalie rushed as she sat up straighter. "That's a great idea."

He hesitated another moment. "I'm not even sure you're

up for it after everything that's happened. You have to still be sore from that fall."

"I'm fine," she insisted. "But rain is supposed to come in later. Will that hurt our chances of Rambo picking up the scent?"

Andrew let out a long breath. "It might. It depends on several factors. How much rain and how long since the man has passed through an area."

"Then it only makes sense that we do this sooner rather than later," Natalie finished.

Andrew couldn't argue with that. She was absolutely correct.

But he still had a lot of reservations about this. It was risky.

Maybe he should go alone.

Yet he knew that Natalie wouldn't go for that. Besides, he didn't want to leave her here by herself.

With a touch of hesitation, he stood. "Okay then. If you're sure you're up for it, then we should get going. The more time that passes, the less likely it is that we'll be able to track the trail. We'll need to pack some water and snacks. You'll need to wear good walking shoes."

Natalie nodded eagerly. "I've got good shoes. Do you have any granola bars? I can grab some of those."

"I do." Andrew told her where to find them. "And there are water bottles in the fridge."

"Okay, I'll pack a couple of those as well."

Fifteen minutes later, they were ready to go.

Numerous scenarios floated through his head. Scenarios he wanted to prepare Natalie for.

What if they found Lexi, but it wasn't the happy ending Natalie desired?

But she already knew the possibilities. He didn't have to voice them out loud.

Maybe he shouldn't have suggested this. Still, there was no way he could talk her out of going now.

Andrew let Rambo sniff Lexi's sweater—Natalie had thought ahead and had grabbed it when she brought her things over from the cabin. The dog needed some kind of scent to follow. And if Lexi had been with the man who'd been at the house, then her scent would most likely be on the man's clothing as well.

He prayed this worked.

Then Andrew gave Rambo the command. "Search!"

It only took the canine a moment to find the trail.

The mountain sloped for the first part of the hike, and the fallen leaves would be slippery and make the trek hazardous. The second part would be a steep incline and equally as challenging, if not more so.

As they passed the area where the man had pushed Natalie off the cliff, Andrew saw her muscles tighten.

She'd been through so much at the hands of this man. How could anyone hate her so much? Exactly what kind of vengeance was this man after? He couldn't imagine Natalie doing anything to upset someone so much.

Andrew would do what he could to keep Natalie out of harm's way, and he prayed he didn't regret this decision.

Natalie's thoughts continued to wander as she and Andrew followed Rambo through the woods.

"Why did he go after Dylan?" she finally asked aloud.

Andrew thought about it a moment before shaking his head. "I don't know. Maybe Dylan discovered something that could lead to Lexi?"

"Maybe. I just can't imagine what it could be."

"Maybe he left here last night and continued looking for Lexi. Maybe he got a little too close to the truth."

They walked for several more minutes as Natalie tried to process that thought.

"What about this pharmaceutical company that the executives worked for?" Andrew said. "Was anyone mad at them?"

"Lots of people. It's a pharmaceutical company. People either worship them for how they've changed their life in a positive way, or they detest them for not living up to their expectations. They have threats made against them on a regular basis."

"Can you remember anyone in particular who may have been upset with them?"

Natalie shook her head. "I wasn't really involved with that side of it. I just worked on the advertising campaigns."

"The operating board members were the ones killed, correct?"

"That's right. It's a large company, and they've recently been expanding. They've since regrouped and hired new people. But I believe most of the operating board was there that night, except for one guy who couldn't make it."

"Do you know if that guy was ever threatened?"

"I'm not sure. Why do you ask?"

"Well, the one guy who couldn't make it could be a suspect."

"That's a possibility. I'd think the police would have checked for an alibi. So you really think this all goes back to Drexel Pharmaceutical?" Natalie studied him as she waited for his answer.

"It seems like a good possibility. Maybe you were lumped in with the rest of them because you were the one who was hoping to promote whatever drug it was."

"I guess that makes sense."

"I mean, the police were so busy focusing on the idea that it could be that one woman's ex-boyfriend that maybe they didn't look in other places."

Natalie chewed on the thought as she walked.

Andrew had a good point.

Maybe they had been looking in the wrong direction this whole time.

What if someone was angry with the pharmaceutical company and anyone associated with it? What if this person wanted to teach them a lesson, and that's why he had come to the dinner and killed everybody?

And afterward…what if this guy couldn't stand the fact that Natalie had gotten away? So he'd tracked her to Gatlinburg and, when he saw Lexi, he assumed that Natalie had simply changed the way she looked.

Then he'd abducted the wrong sister.

By the time he'd realized it, it was too late.

But he knew somehow that Natalie was in town as well. Now he still wanted to finish what he'd started.

And the best way he could do that was by keeping Lexi captive and luring Natalie in?

A shiver raced through Natalie at the thought.

But she very well could be onto something.

Andrew held on to Rambo's leash.

The dog was definitely hot on the trail of *something*.

But he tried not to get his hopes up. Andrew had been in these situations enough to know how this could end. He'd followed scents before only to lose them in parking lots or at roads.

Just as they had when they were looking for Lexi before.

There was a good possibility that could happen now as well.

But they needed to at least explore where this route might take them.

Andrew glanced at his phone again.

There was no service out here in the middle of the mountains, just as he had suspected.

But if they did discover a lead, they'd need to call it in. If this man was as dangerous as Andrew thought he was, then there was no way they could confront him themselves. A situation like that could turn deadly.

The problem was, would Natalie ever go for that? She was determined to find and help her sister. Which he understood, of course. But there would come a point where backup would be necessary.

Rambo hadn't lost the scent yet.

"I have to admit, Rambo is a pretty great dog," Natalie said.

"He is. He's great at what he does. He's found missing hikers. People involved in abductions. He's the real hero here." Andrew rubbed the dog's head affectionately.

"I think that's great that the two of you have such a good bond."

Suddenly, Rambo turned and headed back north.

"Where's he going?" Natalie asked.

"He caught the scent of something."

Ten minutes later, Lexi's cabin appeared.

"Wait…why did he bring us back here?" Disappointment rang through Natalie's voice.

"He must have a reason. What is it, Rambo?"

The dog pulled on the leash harder and faster.

As they reached the back of the cabin, Andrew saw someone lying unmoving near the door.

Natalie gasped. "Lexi?"

Then she darted toward the woman lying on the porch.

TWENTY-TWO

Natalie rushed to her sister.

Was she dead?

Her heart pounded with fear.

No…

She knelt beside her and shook her. "Lexi?"

But she didn't move. Her eyes were bruised, her lip busted and her hair matted.

Andrew appeared beside her and pressed his finger into her neck. "She still has a pulse."

"What did that man do to her?"

"I don't know, but he must have just left here not long ago. She wasn't here when Caruso and his guys checked this place out. Let's get her inside."

Andrew handed Rambo's leash to Natalie. Then he lifted Lexi into his arms and carried her to the door.

Natalie unlocked it, her hands trembling. Then she held the door open.

Andrew rushed inside and laid Lexi on the couch.

As he did, Lexi let out a moan.

Natalie's breath caught. Maybe she was okay! "Lexi, it's me. You're back home. You're safe now."

Why would this guy just return her? Why now?

Regardless of the answer, Natalie was thankful to have her sister back.

She glanced at Andrew.

He had his cell phone out and placed to his ear as he explained to emergency services what was happening.

"Lexi, can you hear me?" Natalie leaned over her sister. "Help is coming."

She thrashed her head back and forth and moaned again.

Good. She was coming to. Maybe she would wake up and tell them what had happened to her.

But those bruises…

A knot lodged in Natalie's throat.

She didn't even want to imagine what her sister had been through.

Suddenly, Lexi's eyes flung open.

She reached for Natalie and gripped her arm so tightly that Natalie flinched.

"Natalie…" Lexi stared at her.

"I'm here."

"I need…help."

"We called 911. They are on their way. It's going to be okay."

Lexi shook her head. "No, you don't understand. I… I need…money."

"What? Money? Why do you need money?"

What exactly had Lexi gotten herself into?

Andrew didn't like the sound of this.

More and more tension twisted his muscles.

Natalie managed to help Lexi sit up. She didn't appear to have any broken bones—though she'd obviously been through a terrible ordeal.

He grabbed her a glass of water and waited for her to take a sip before asking any questions.

Lexi handed the glass back to Andrew, and he set it on the end table.

"You said you need money?" he asked.

Lexi nodded. "A lot of money. I… I messed up."

"What do you mean you messed up?" Natalie asked after lowering herself onto the couch beside Lexi. "What's really going on here?"

Lexi ran a hand through her hair. "I'm in trouble. Real trouble."

"What are you talking about?" Natalie leaned closer.

Lexi's eyes glazed again. "I owe someone a lot of money. If I don't pay him…he'll be back. And next time… he'll kill me."

"Did you borrow money from someone?" Andrew stepped closer. He didn't like the sound of this.

"I didn't borrow anything." Lexi's gaze flickered up to Andrew and then back to her sister. "I got myself into some bad stuff."

"Lexi, you're going to have to be more specific," Natalie said.

Lexi glanced at her hands and wobbled.

Andrew feared she might pass out again. "Do you need to lie down?"

Lexi waved them off. "I don't have time to lie down."

"You have to tell us more, Lexi." Natalie stared at her sister, waiting for her to continue. "We want to help you."

"I…stole some drugs from someone."

"What?" Natalie gasped.

"I know. I shouldn't have." Lexi pressed her eyes closed. "But I needed money and…"

"You thought stealing drugs was the answer?" Andrew finished, trying to keep any judgment from his voice. "Were you planning to sell them?"

"I…was already selling them for this guy."

"The guy you stole from?" Andrew looked at Natalie. "That must be the side gig that Dylan had told us about."

"Oh, Lexi. Why? Why would you get involved in something like that?" Natalie shook her head.

"I needed the money, okay? I don't have a fancy job like you do! You don't get it, do you? You don't know what it's like to struggle every day to pay the mortgage. To put food on the table."

"Lexi, why didn't you come to me?"

"We weren't exactly close, were we?"

Andrew knew there wasn't time to get into the details of their relationship. "Stay on track, Lexi. What did you need the money for specifically?"

"I maxed out my credit cards, okay? They were going to take my house. With all the interest, there was no way I could pay off my bills on what I make at the Bistro. So in addition to selling for this guy, I started stealing some of his drugs. I figured I could sell what he gave me and give him his cut. Then I could sell what I'd taken and keep all the profits."

"You thought you'd scam a drug dealer? What were you thinking?"

"I... I just took a little at first. And he didn't seem to notice. So I just took a little more..."

"And he eventually found out?"

She nodded. "He wasn't happy...to say the least."

"I can imagine he wasn't," Andrew said. "Tell us what happened next."

As Lexi became a little more aware, she looked at Andrew and narrowed her eyes. "Wait. What are you even doing here? I know you're a cop. You're just trying to get information out of me so you can arrest me, aren't you?"

"Lexi!" Natalie cut in. "That's not it at all. We are both only trying to help you."

"She's right. That's not what this is about," Andrew added. "I'm taking a leave of absence. I'm not here to get you in trouble. I...care about your sister. I'm trying to help both of you."

Lexi looked doubtful but, after a moment, nodded. "When I got off work a couple of nights ago, I walked to my car and heard someone crying for help in the woods. I knew I should have ignored it, but I couldn't just leave them there. When I went into the woods, someone grabbed me."

"Lexi…" Natalie squeezed her hand.

Andrew kept an eye out for any police vehicles that were headed their way. He wanted to get to the bottom of this before Caruso arrived and took over the scene.

"The guy, he kept demanding I give the drugs back or give him the money I made from selling them." Her voice trembled. "I told him the drugs are gone. I sold them all. I don't have the money anymore either. I used it to pay off some of my debts."

"Oh, Lexi," Natalie whispered.

"He didn't believe me. He kept pushing me to tell him where I'd hidden the cash."

"Which is why he tore up the cushions of your car seats…" Natalie murmured. "He thought you might have hidden the money in your car."

"Why did he let you go?" Andrew asked.

"Because I told him if he did I'd get the money for him." Her eyes glazed again. "I promised him double what I took from him."

"Who is this guy?"

"I can't tell you. He threatened me. Told me I couldn't tell anyone who he is."

"You can tell us," Natalie said. "You have to. We need to bring this guy down."

"No! I can't give you his name. He's too connected. He would find out. Can't you just pay him? Please? I'll pay you back." Desperation lined her voice. "I promise. I'll work two jobs if I have to."

Natalie and Andrew exchanged a glance.

"I'm not sure that's a good idea," Andrew finally said.

"But he'll kill me…" A cry escaped from Lexi, and her skin went pale.

Natalie scooted closer. "Who is it, Lexi? Just tell us so we can help you."

"You wouldn't even believe me if I told you." Tears welled and spilled down her cheeks.

"Try us," Andrew said.

"He…he has ears everywhere. I can't escape him." Her gaze met Andrew's. "You can't stop him either. No one can."

This guy really had a hold on Lexi, didn't he? He'd made her think there was no other option than to do what he said.

"You don't know that. Let us help." Andrew leaned closer. "Who is it?"

Lexi started to say something, but before she could answer, her eyes rolled back, and she collapsed onto the couch.

Natalie felt panic racing through her. "Lexi!"

Andrew quickly laid her flat. "I think she just passed out. We need to get her to the hospital."

Just in time, sirens sounded in the distance.

Andrew stepped outside to flag the ambulance down while Natalie tried to wake up her sister.

"Lexi…what did you get yourself into?"

There were two separate crimes going on here, Natalie realized. When the man had sounded confused earlier when she'd mentioned him taking her sister, that was because he hadn't taken Lexi. He'd been telling the truth.

They were far from being out of danger, weren't they?

But who exactly was this drug dealer who had abducted Lexi? Somebody with connections?

Could it be someone she worked with at the restaurant?

But if so, why did Lexi think the person was untouchable?

There were still too many unanswered questions right now.

At Andrew's direction, the paramedics rushed inside, and Natalie moved out of the way as they began to work on Lexi.

Andrew joined Natalie and slid his arm around her waist comfortingly. She leaned into him, grateful for his presence.

"We're going to take her to the hospital," the paramedics said after taking her vitals and getting her situated on a gurney. "You can meet us there."

Natalie nodded, her eyes full of unshed tears.

She watched her sister being taken away and prayed for her safety.

If this man truly did have connections, what if he tried to find her in the hospital?

That made it even more urgent that she follow behind.

"We need to go. She needs someone looking out for her."

Andrew nodded. "I understand."

She knew the police were on their way and that they would also want to take a statement from each of them. But the cops could wait.

First, she wanted to make sure her sister was okay.

TWENTY-THREE

Andrew wished he'd thought to ask for a ride back to his place. But he hadn't, and the paramedics were gone.

The police would take their statements at the hospital.

But that meant that he, Natalie and Rambo would need to walk back to his place to get a vehicle since that was where they had all been left.

He could sense Natalie was distressed as they walked.

Not only that, but he had to keep his eyes wide open right now.

He now knew that they were facing an unknown drug dealer in addition to the person who was taunting Natalie. He hadn't been able to dissect the two crimes yet, to know which perpetrator had executed which crime. He could only guess that the man coming after Natalie had left the peanut dust and the threatening messages to her.

The man at the cabin the first night…he very well could've been the man who had abducted Lexi. Perhaps he had come back to look for the money at her place.

They still had a lot of unanswered questions.

His thoughts raced through everything that had happened as they walked through the darkness.

Natalie shivered beside him.

"It's going to be okay," he murmured.

And it would be. One way or another.

But he wasn't sure what they would have to go through to get to that point of being okay. There was still a lot of danger out there that they needed to overcome.

"Thank you for all your help," Natalie finally said.

"Of course. Whatever I can do."

"We're not out of danger yet, are we?"

He pressed his lips together, his jaw thumping. "No, unfortunately, we're not."

"I wonder who this drug dealer is."

"I've been thinking about that also. I don't know. My thoughts keep going back to Frank. He had that nice car in his driveway even though he lived in a house that was rather run-down. He would have connections."

"And why did Dylan die?" Natalie asked.

"I have a feeling he was involved in all of this also. Maybe he didn't know exactly who the drug dealer was, but I think he was helping your sister. Maybe this guy got to him and tried to demand he tell him where any money or drugs are being kept. But when Dylan told him it was all gone…"

"It's a solid theory. It doesn't surprise me at all that Lexi would have needed that money to pay off her debts. I'm sure she's in debt because she likes to live a lavish lifestyle. She likes brand-name items. Purses. Clothes. Shoes. She always has had expensive tastes. Her choice to sell drugs? It explains why she bought this cabin out here. It's easier to do things under the cover of darkness."

His gut tightened. "Yes, it sure is."

Finally, he spotted his cabin in the distance.

"I'll grab my purse and keys. Then we'll take off for the hospital." Natalie's gaze caught his. "I want to be there when Lexi wakes up. I want to talk to her."

"Of course."

They reached his house and stepped inside.

"I'll be right back," Natalie said before hurrying toward the guest bedroom. Her voice trembled as she said the words. She was obviously on edge.

Andrew glanced at a package of something sticking out from beneath a couch cushion and sucked in a breath. What was that?

It hadn't been there when they'd left.

Carefully, he pulled it out.

His breath whooshed out from his lungs when he recognized what was in his hands.

It was a brick of heroin.

How had this gotten here?

When Rambo growled, Andrew knew they weren't alone.

He looked up when Natalie stepped out of the spare bedroom. Her face was pale, and she hadn't picked up her purse or keys.

"Natalie, what's wrong?"

That's when a man wearing a mask appeared behind her, his gun aimed at Natalie's head.

Natalie felt the gun pressing into her temple.

The man.

He was here.

He'd been just waiting for them to return.

Now he was going to finish what he started two months ago.

Uncontrollable quivers wracked her body.

"Put your gun on the ground and kick it toward me!" the man grumbled. "Now!"

Andrew did as he asked, the gun skittering across the floor. "You don't have to do this."

"Sure, I do. I've come too far to back out now."

Rambo continued to growl.

"Put the dog in the bathroom and close the door," the man said. "Don't make me tell you twice."

Andrew raised his hands. "Don't get upset. I'll put him away."

Carefully, Andrew skirted around Natalie and the gunman, leading Rambo into the bathroom and shutting the door, just as the man had told him.

"I used to have a dog, also," the man said. "He was my pride and joy."

"Was?" Natalie asked.

"Unfortunately, he died not long ago. Had a tumor. I miss him. He was the one who inspired my company." Grief sounded in his voice—grief mixed with anger.

"Is this dog you lost the German shepherd that you had attack me?" Natalie's throat burned as she said the words.

A sly grin slid across his face. "The one and only. You know, I rewarded him with a steak after we left you there. Imagine my surprise when I learned you had survived. Oh well, it worked out in the end, didn't it? You had to suffer through recovery. Then you had to live in fear for all this time. It turned out quite brilliantly, if I do say so myself."

"You call what you've been doing to me all this time brilliant?"

Sadistic was more like it.

But she wasn't about to say that aloud.

"You deserved everything you got. You might have everyone else fooled, but not me. I know you're cold and heartless deep down." He shoved the gun harder against Natalie's temple. "You don't care about anything but your bottom line, do you?"

"I don't know what you're talking about." Natalie's voice quivered. This guy wasn't right in the head.

The man suddenly shoved her away toward Andrew. Now they were both facing him, and the barrel of his gun.

Again he wore all black. A black mask also covered his face.

"Maybe when this is all done, I'll take your dog instead." An evil glimmer entered his eyes as he turned to Andrew. "Every dog can be trained to kill."

Natalie saw the veins popping out on Andrew's neck. "We need to talk this through."

The man aimed the gun directly at Natalie's head again. "There's nothing else to talk through. I've been looking forward to this moment for a long time now. I've tried many times. Too many times. And finally, here we are. Nothing is going to stop me from getting what I want."

"How is killing me going to help anything?" Natalie's thoughts raced. "What exactly is it that you want?"

"Don't you know?" he asked. "Those other people at the pharmaceutical company…they weren't my targets. You were."

All the blood drained from her face, and she felt like she could pass out. "What do you mean? Are you saying you killed them because I was going to be there? You were looking for me?"

"You really don't know?"

"I have no idea what you're talking about or what I could've done to make you this angry."

Still aiming the gun at her head, he jerked his mask off.

She gasped when she saw the familiar face staring at her. In all her imagining who this man could possibly be, this guy had never crossed her mind.

"Burke Snyder?"

He scowled. "So you do remember me."

"Of course I remember you. But…why? Why kill all those people? Why come after me?"

The man had wanted to hire her to do the advertising campaign for his startup company Sent Scent. But he hadn't had the budget for what he'd wanted, and he hadn't been willing to scale back and compromise. Besides that, the project hadn't really interested her. So Natalie had turned him down.

"I had to shut my company down six months ago," he growled. "My dreams all died. If I'd just been able to spread the word about my product, it *would* have been a success. I can promise you that. But my whole life fell apart after you refused to create a campaign for me."

"There were other avenues you could've explored. Other advertising agencies."

"None like yours. You were the best. You ruined me! I invested everything in that company. I spent so much time working on my product that my wife left me and took the kids with her. The company was all I had left."

"Not every product was a good fit for the company," Natalie explained, knowing her words would fall on deaf ears.

She had to think of something to distract Burke. Maybe then Andrew could disarm the guy. But what could she do that wouldn't end in someone being shot?

"You took on that pharmaceutical company instead of my company, even though they could be unethical and charge exorbitant prices for their products." He spat out the words with so much force that moisture hit Natalie's ear. "Don't you know what it means to support small businesses? Businesses that regular people like me rely on for their income?"

"It wasn't personal," she said. "It was business."

"I hate it when people say that! It was personal to me! That's why I need to make sure that you lose everything… just like I did."

"You know I'm not working for that company anymore, don't you?" Natalie said as her thoughts raced. She needed to figure out a way to stop him.

He sneered. "So you lost your job. That's not enough. That's just the start of it. Now I need to take away everything that you care about. I should've just ended it last night on the cliff. I should've shot you and then pushed you over. But I didn't. I realize now what a mistake that was."

"You're the man I saw watching me across the street at the restaurant, aren't you?"

He smirked. "I am. I knew you were in this area, but I couldn't figure out where exactly. Then I spotted you eating. I felt like I'd hit the jackpot."

"And you discovered my new cell phone number and sent me that message?"

"I had it all typed out before that guy started to chase me. All I had to do was hit Send as soon as I got in my car. I thought the message would be effective and keep you on edge. It looks like I was right."

"Then you left the peanut dust in the tea—because you found out about that also. And you tried to lure me into the woods to get me away from Andrew. You watched my sister as she worked in the restaurant, didn't you?"

He shrugged. "At first, I thought it was you. Then I realized it wasn't and left her alone."

"Were you the one who nearly ran us off the road?"

"I'm afraid I can't claim that one. But I saw that other guy watching you. I knew I had some competition. I thought about taking him out of the picture, but then thought it might be entertaining to watch and see what he did."

"What other guy?" This had to be the man who'd taken Lexi. The drug dealer. "What did he look like?"

"I'm not telling you," he scoffed. "What does it matter anyway? It's not like you're going to live long enough to do anything about it."

Natalie's thoughts continued to race. This man was off balance, to say the least.

Her gut told her time was running out.

What was she going to do?

She exchanged a glance with Andrew and prayed he had a better plan than she did, because as of now, she didn't have a plan at all.

Andrew knew that he had to do something, or this was going to have an ugly ending.

Rambo continued to bark in the bathroom and claw at the door.

At least the dog was better off in the safety of the closed room. But the thought of this man turning his dog into some kind of killing machine made anger surge through him.

Rambo was his dog. Nobody was going to take him away.

The guy was obviously off-kilter. Something wasn't right with him.

But right now, the man had a gun aimed at Natalie's head. With that in mind, Andrew would need to proceed with caution.

"Why don't you just let us talk this through?" Andrew said, keeping his voice calm.

"I don't want to talk anymore!" The man's nostrils flared. "I just need this woman to pay for what happened."

"You've already taken eight lives," Andrew said. "Why take one more?"

"Because she was the target all along. Or weren't you listening a bit ago when I explained it all? Nobody listens to me. That's the problem, isn't it? No one appreciates me or my ideas!"

"Killing Natalie won't solve anything."

"Maybe not, but it'll sure make *me* feel better." He jabbed a finger into his own chest.

"Not when you're in jail. You've already lost so much. Do you really want to add your freedom to that list?"

His eyes narrowed with vengeance. "That would require

me being caught first. I'm not going to let that happen. I'm too smart for that. I have it all planned out."

"What are you planning to do?" Andrew asked, trying to buy more time.

"You'll find out soon enough."

"How did you even find me here?" Natalie's voice trembled as she asked the question. "I was careful not to let anyone follow me. I changed my phone number."

"I used a product I developed when I worked for the tech company. I programmed a code on your smart watch, and it let me know where you were."

"That's an invasion of privacy," Andrew told him. "And illegal."

Sure, it paled in comparison to murdering eight people, and attempting to murder Natalie. But he wanted to keep the man talking. He needed time to think of a way out of this.

"It was brilliant! I don't want to hear your opinion!" The man's voice rose. "Now, let's just get this over with."

"What if it's not too late?" Natalie suddenly spoke up. "The idea for your business. I could work with you on an advertising campaign at no charge. How does that sound? You could start again. I could help you restart your business. Everyone would know then that you're not a failure. Your ideas are solid. Your products would be sold all over the world."

Andrew knew Natalie was grasping for ideas here. But judging by the wild look in this man's eyes, he was beyond convincing of anything.

He looked at Natalie. "Come back over here. It's time to end this."

Andrew shook his head. "You don't want to do this."

But the man stepped forward and grabbed Natalie again, pressing the gun to her head.

TWENTY-FOUR

Natalie felt more panic racing through her.

This guy was just agitated enough to actually pull the trigger.

And she was at his mercy right now.

Andrew was a far enough distance away that there would be no way he could tackle this guy before he could shoot.

So what were they going to do?

"Killing her isn't going to solve any of your problems," Andrew said. "It will only make things worse. You still aren't going to have your company back, or your family. But if you don't hurt her, you still have a chance of doing something good with your life and turning things around."

"No! It's too late. It's too late for it all."

As his grip on her arm tightened, Natalie braced herself.

At any moment, he could discharge his weapon.

She could sense his anger rising, and knew it was only a matter of time.

She pressed her eyes shut.

Lord, I am so sorry that it took me this long to turn back to You. I'm sorry it took tragedy for me to realize that I can't do life on my own.

She opened her eyes and stared at Andrew, trying to

silently convey to him how much she appreciated everything that he had done for her.

If they had had the chance, they could've had something beautiful together.

She realized with clarity just how true that thought was.

"Sorry, it had to end this way," the man muttered, his words sounding eerily final.

She squeezed her eyes shut again as she braced herself for the oncoming pain.

"Release!" Andrew yelled.

Burke's eyes widened with confusion.

Andrew knew that he was out of time. He had to do something. Now.

The next instant, the bathroom door flew open, and Rambo barged out.

In the blink of an eye, he tackled the gunman to the ground.

The gun scattered across the floor, and Andrew grabbed it. Then he called Rambo off, flipped the man over and pressed his knee into his back.

"Natalie, give me the zip ties out of that drawer over there."

She came out of her state of shock and quickly scrambled across the room. She grabbed the zip ties, and then Andrew bound this man's wrists together behind him.

"Good boy," Andrew murmured, giving Rambo a pat on the head.

"He opened the door…" Natalie muttered, a touch of awe in her voice. "That's amazing."

"Dogs are amazing creatures." He stood and jerked the man to his feet. "It's over, Burke. You won't be hurting anybody else."

He grabbed his phone and called 911, but the dispatcher said the police were already on their way.

When Andrew and Natalie hadn't shown up at the hospital, Caruso had decided to send someone out for them.

Maybe Natalie could finally rest assured she was safe.

The only problem left was Lexi. She still owed somebody money. That meant danger could still be following her.

Andrew's gut tensed. He didn't like the thought of that. He just wanted all of this to be over.

He scowled at Burke again, unable to believe the lengths this guy had gone to just to get what he perceived as revenge.

Natalie also stared at him with contempt.

"This isn't the end of it," Burke promised as he sneered at them. "I'll still figure out a way to get you back. You're not the only one with connections."

"We'll see about that," Andrew said as he shoved Burke onto the couch. The man was just blowing smoke. Maybe he had convinced himself nobody could stop him. But it was too late. His reign of terror was finally over.

A moment later, a knock sounded at the door.

Natalie crossed the room and opened it.

Caruso stood on the doorstep.

He was alone.

"What's going on?" His gaze went to Burke.

They quickly gave him an update on the situation.

"Well, I'm glad you guys are okay," Caruso said as he strode toward Burke. "We're going to have more questions for you, of course."

"Of course," Andrew said. "I thought you were sending some of your patrol officers over here."

Caruso shrugged. "I figured I'd come out here myself. Sometimes to get a job done right, you've got to do it yourself."

Just before Caruso reached Burke, he grabbed the gun from his holster and shot the man twice in his chest.

Burke fell over and slid to the floor.

Andrew bristled and reached for his own gun.

Before he could grab it, Caruso aimed his weapon toward Andrew. "I wouldn't do that. Take it out slowly. Put it on the floor."

Andrew knew he had no choice but to do that.

"You were the guy all along," Natalie said breathlessly. "The drug dealer. You were the one calling the shots with my sister."

"She owes me money. I need it."

"How can you even call yourself a cop and do this?" Andrew muttered as disgust roiled inside him.

"You have no room to talk. You take bribes. You're as crooked as I am. Besides, it's none of your business. I have my reasons."

Andrew should have seen this. He should have been able to put it together. But now everything made so much sense.

"How much money does she owe you?"

"Nearly a half million," Caruso said. "Maybe she doesn't have it. But I know Natalie does."

"I don't have that kind of money," Natalie said. "What makes you think that?"

"I know about that cushy job you had. I've seen your nice car. I even looked up your condo that you sold, and I know how much you made from it. I'm not stupid. So stop playing games with me."

"I still owed a lot on my mortgage. I didn't make all that much in profit. Even if I did have that kind of money, it would take a long time for me to be able to withdraw those funds. You're a cop, you know that."

"I have some time to kill." Caruso shrugged.

"You don't think your colleagues are going to question what's taking you so long?" Andrew asked, his thoughts continuing to race. He needed to find a way to throw Caruso off his game.

Something to sideline him. But what?

"I told them I had to track down another lead," Caruso said. "That will buy me some time."

Rambo growled behind him, and Andrew feared for the dog's safety—as well as Natalie's.

"Heel, Rambo. Heel."

"Give me your passwords," Caruso demanded.

"What?"

"To your bank accounts. I'm going to get the money myself. I'll take as much time as I need."

"You know it's not that easy," Natalie told him. "There are two-step verifications in place. You can't just log on from any device."

"I'll figure something out. Now write them down!"

"Okay." Natalie grabbed some paper from a table and a pen. Then she began writing everything he'd demanded.

"You're going to kill us, aren't you? Just like you killed Burke." Andrew nodded at the dead man on the floor. "How are you going to explain three dead people?"

"I'll say that things turned hostile. That I came here to check out a lead and found the drugs you'd taken. You pulled a gun on me. I had no choice but to fire back."

"Wait. Drugs?" Natalie murmured. What was he talking about?

"That's right. He didn't tell you?" Caruso smirked.

Andrew turned toward her. "Someone planted drugs here while we were gone. Caruso wanted to set me up."

She jerked her gaze back to the cop. "You give police a bad name."

"I put my life on the line every day for other people and never get any appreciation. I get cursed at, harassed, and work with people who do nothing but complain and make my life miserable. I definitely don't make enough money for this gig. So I decided to look for other means to make some cash. With my contacts at the police department, I could easily sweep things under the rug. And I was doing a fine job at it, until your sister screwed things up."

"You screwed things up for yourself. You sold your soul to the devil," Andrew murmured, disgust in his voice.

"I did what I had to do to get what I deserved. But once I researched you and realized the hot water you were in back in Nashville, I knew you'd make the perfect scapegoat."

"You make me sick." Andrew shook his head. "You deserve to be behind bars."

Caruso shrugged and looked back at Natalie. "Did you finish writing down the account information and passwords?"

She nodded.

She met Andrew's gaze and held it for a moment. Just long enough to convey that she had an idea.

He gave her a slight, barely perceptible nod.

Natalie turned to Caruso and held out the paper. "Here it is."

But when he went to grab the paper, she dropped it.

He reached for it, the motion surprising him.

And it gave Andrew just enough time to grab him. To twist the gun out of his hand.

Caruso's gun dropped to the floor and slid under the couch as they continued struggling.

Caruso's gun was out of reach. But Burke's wasn't.

Natalie backed away and scooped up Burke's gun.

She raised it. "Back off, Caruso!"

The detective froze as he looked up at her. "You don't have the nerve to pull the trigger."

"Don't test me," she murmured.

"You can shoot me, but you won't kill me. You don't have it in you. I'll deny everything. It'll be my word against yours. A failed advertising executive versus a respected police detective? Who do you think will win?" Caruso turned to Andrew. "And you? A fallen cop? One who takes bribes." He nodded toward the brick of heroin he'd planted. "And how are you going to explain that?"

"You're grasping at straws, Detective." Natalie shook her head. "I'll tell your superiors about how you stole drugs from evidence. How you sold them on the streets. What about the fact you abducted my sister and beat her? I'll tell them how you killed Dylan. How you shot Burke in cold blood before he could even explain himself. He even had his hands secured behind his back. How are you going to weasel your way out of that fact?"

"They won't believe anything you say."

"I think they will," Andrew murmured. "The evidence will speak for itself."

"I know how to explain away evidence. This isn't my first rodeo."

"It's not mine either," Andrew reminded him as he crossed his arms and stood there.

Something about his voice and his confident stance made Natalie wonder.

Did he have another plan?

Just then, more police barged in.

Not the local cops. Their uniforms were different colors.

"Tennessee Bureau of Investigation," one of the men shouted. "Drop your weapons and hands up!"

Natalie did as the man instructed and glanced at Andrew.

He'd figured this might happen, hadn't he? He'd already called this in and asked them to come.

This man was fast becoming her real-life hero. Him and his dog Rambo.

As they handcuffed Caruso and took him away, Natalie realized that justice might finally be served.

* * *

Andrew stared across the room at Natalie as a smile bloomed across her beautiful face.

As soon as the police were distracted with analyzing the crime scene, he stepped toward her, and she fell into his arms.

"I'm so glad you're okay," he said.

"I wasn't sure about anything there for a while." She nestled into him.

"It was rough."

She nodded in agreement.

Just then, Rambo jumped up on them as if he wanted to be included in the hug.

Andrew and Natalie both laughed and stepped away from each other and patted him on the head also.

Natalie even knelt beside the dog and wrapped her arms around him. "You're my favorite dog ever, Rambo. You can have my back anytime."

Andrew was delighted to see that she no longer seemed to be afraid of his dog. Maybe now that Rambo had saved them, she could see that not all dogs were scary.

"Time's up, Rambo." He gave Natalie a hand up and tugged her into his arms again. "It's my turn."

She met his gaze. "I can't believe this all just happened," she murmured. "First Burke and then Caruso. This whole time I was looking in the wrong direction. I mean, I suspected maybe there were two different scenarios going on here, but I didn't know for sure. And this guy Burke? I knew he was upset, but it never crossed my mind he would resort to this. To kill so many people…"

"None of this is your fault, you know that, right?"

She nodded. "I do know. I just don't understand how he could take this to such extreme lengths. And then Caruso… It's going to take me some time to sort all this out."

"You couldn't have known who was doing what. There

was a lot going on. We would have gotten to the truth eventually. Unfortunately, it had to come down to this first."

"What do you think is going to happen to Caruso?"

"He's going to be going away for a long time. The evidence against him is irrefutable."

"And Lexi? Do you think she'll go to jail?"

"I'm not sure. She may just get a probation period. It's hard to say. I hate to say it like this, but maybe prison would be a good wakeup call for her. If she went, she probably wouldn't serve long."

Natalie nodded and didn't deny what he said. "So you called the TBI earlier?"

"I did. I began to suspect that maybe Caruso was involved. It was mostly a gut feeling, but the way he was acting bugged me, made me think he was hiding something. Most cops don't date people who might be in the drug scene."

"Good point."

"I didn't know he was going to come here tonight, however. Thankfully, the officers outside heard most of our conversation. They were just waiting for the right time to act. We have witnesses to corroborate everything that went down."

"That's a relief." She turned and looked at the couch and the floor where there was still blood from where Burke had been shot. "This didn't have to happen."

"I'm sorry it ended that way," Andrew said. "But I'm glad that you won't have to worry about him anymore. The man was obviously delusional."

"Yes, he was. As I mentioned, it's going to take me a while to comprehend everything that just happened. But I already feel relief from the constant fear I was experiencing."

"Now that this is over, do you think you'll go back to Cincinnati and take up your old job again?" Andrew held his breath as he waited for her answer. "I know you enjoy living in the city."

"I do." She shrugged. "But I've been thinking about that. When I started thinking about returning to the grind, to the way I was living… I realized that my work was my life. I'm not sure that's what I want anymore. There's so much more to experience. It's all about finding that balance, you know?" She stared up at him. "What about you? What are you going to do? Are you going back to Nashville?"

"The people in the department turned on me quickly. They might've been my colleagues, but they were never truly my friends. I know I'm not guilty, and they will find out I'm not one day, but I'm not sure if I can ever trust any of them again."

"What else would you do if you don't go back there?"

He stared out the door at the police lights flashing there. "Well, it looks like there's going to be an opening for another detective in Gatlinburg pretty soon."

A smile stretched across her face. "Now that you mention it, it does look like they are going to be one detective short after tonight. I'd be glad to give you a glowing reference if you need one. You did save my life after all. You and your faithful companion."

"I might just take you up on that offer." Andrew grinned as he leaned forward and planted a slow, lingering kiss on her lips. One that he hoped was the first of many to come.

EPILOGUE

One Month Later

"Come here, boy!" Natalie patted her leg.

Rambo bounded toward her, his tongue hanging out. She rewarded his obedience with a nice, long head rub.

Andrew caught up with them and smiled. "I didn't realize the two of you would be so excited to take this hike."

"It's a beautiful day so we might as well enjoy it."

A lot had happened since Caruso had been arrested.

Lexi had been kept in the hospital for two days before being released and put directly into rehab. She was able to make a deal. If she testified against Caruso, then the charges against her were going to be dropped.

Back in Nashville, Sarah had tried everything she could to convince Andrew to move back and marry her. She'd said they'd been through too much to just throw everything away.

Andrew had reminded her that she was the one who'd destroyed their relationship, and their future. He'd made it clear that there would be no turning back.

She'd pleaded her case with her dad, but as she was spinning lies, he'd caught on to the fact that each time she told her story it changed a little bit. He'd finally gotten fed up with her cajoling, and he'd insisted she take a lie detector test.

She'd refused at first, and then, threatened with the possibility of losing her inheritance, she'd promptly confessed that she had planted the drugs in Andrew's locker to make him look guilty. His name had been cleared and he was offered his job back.

But he had declined the offer.

Instead he had applied to work at the Gatlinburg PD.

He was offered the job with a sizable sign-on bonus for his help in bringing down Caruso. He would be starting next week.

Last he'd heard, Sarah had already started dating some other guy and had moved on. Again.

Natalie had decided that she didn't want to go back to the grind of working as an advertising executive. Instead, she opened her own business and became an advertising consultant. She would now be working at home with flexible hours.

She was currently staying at Lexi's place and fixing it up a little. Once Lexi was out of rehab, Natalie would figure out an alternate plan. But for now, it was working out just fine with her, and she was enjoying having Andrew and Rambo so close by.

Andrew's cabin had been cleaned and scrubbed and there was no longer any evidence of what had happened there. The police had confirmed that Burke was behind everything. They'd found irrefutable evidence at his home and had put the case to rest. At least now the families of the victims could have a little peace of mind knowing that the person responsible for those deaths was no longer a threat.

It was proven Dylan had been killed by Caruso. Caruso had confessed to that while he was being interrogated.

Andrew was correct when he'd said that Caruso would

not be seeing freedom for a very long time. He had multiple charges against him. The evidence was overwhelming.

Natalie still marveled at the two separate crimes that had been going on, but she was so thankful that it was finally now over.

Now that Lexi was in rehab, Natalie was hopeful that her sister would finally turn her life around. She hadn't been able to talk to Lexi since she'd gone into the program. But she planned on trying to rebuild the close relationship they'd once had.

"I think Lexi's going to be okay," Natalie announced.

Andrew took her hand in his as they continued to walk on the beautiful mountain trail. "I hope so. You two need each other in your lives."

"I know a couple of others that I need in my life also." She squeezed his hand and glanced at Rambo as he trotted along beside them.

"That's good. Because we need you too."

Tennessee and these wonderful Smoky Mountains that had once been intended as their temporary respite would now become both of their homes.

Natalie felt certain that she and Andrew had more in store for their future.

She could easily see her life with Andrew, and she knew he felt the same.

But they didn't want to rush anything. They would take time to heal. To get to know each other, and to revel in their newfound happiness.

Rambo, on the other hand, was ready to jump in with all four paws. He would join Andrew working with the Gatlinburg PD and spend the rest of his days doing what he did best—protecting and serving.

* * * * *

Dear Reader,

Thank you so much for reading *Lethal Mountain Pursuit*. I hope you enjoyed Natalie, Andrew and Rambo's story, as well as the beautiful Smoky Mountains setting. There's something about the Tennessee mountains that I just love.

In the book, both Natalie and Andrew are struggling with things that happened in their pasts. I think this is something we can all relate with—but hopefully not to the same extreme. Our pasts can help shape us into the people we are, but the past doesn't have to define us. Sometimes, it simply creates obstacles to overcome. Those obstacles can ultimately help us grow stronger.

Always remember that the Lord is faithful and that He'll protect us, whatever comes our way.

Blessings,

Christy Barritt